Horror Stories: A Short Story Collection

Written by Ron Ripley, David Longhorn, Eric Whittle,
Sara Clancy and A.I. Nasser
Edited by Emma Salam

ISBN-13: 978-1539759102
ISBN-10: 1539759105

Thank You and Bonus Novel!

We'd like to take a moment to thank you for your ongoing support. You make this all possible! To really show you our appreciation for purchasing this book, we've included a bonus scene at the end of this book. **We'd also love to send you the full length novel: Sherman's Library Trilogy in 3 formats (MOBI, EPUB and PDF) absolutely free!**

Download Sherman's Library Trilogy in 3 formats, get FREE short stories, and receive future discounts by visiting www.ScareStreet.com

Keeping it spooky,
Team Scare Street

Table of Contents

Going for a Walk
By Ron Ripley

Night had fallen, and the air was cool. A few birds continued to sing from their nests in the tall pines along the roadside. Wendy's footsteps were loud in her ears as she walked. The road was unfamiliar to her, as was the neighborhood, itself. Her new apartment was two miles back the way she had come, and she still had another mile to go before she reached her turn-around point. She kept a steady pace, her fanny-pack bouncing rhythmically against her behind.

The occasional car raced past, some of them moving away from the shoulder of the road and others staying close. Wendy's reflective safety vest and blinking light seemed only to alert the drivers who were actually paying attention to the road. It was a roll of the dice whether or not she would be hit every time a car came by, but she didn't mind.

The weather was pleasant, and it was good to get outside, away from her computer and the constant research.

She began whistling to herself as she approached the closed off road to an old campground. A rusting chain stretched across the cracked pavement of the entrance was looped around two pine trees. From the chain's sagging center, a faded sign reading "No Trespassing" hung limply.

There was no breeze to move it. As Wendy drew closer, she heard a curious sound. Almost as though someone, or something, was shuffling towards her. When she reached the entrance, she paused and looked down the dark road. The alternating flash of red and white from her safety light illuminated the trees in a harsh way, giving the tree-lined passage a nightmarish quality.

And Wendy saw movement.

A large hunched over shape. It took her a moment to realize it was a person, one dressed in rags and with a backpack on. The stranger shuffled towards her, caught sight of the light and lifted its head up.

From the depths of the hood, long, stringy white hair fell down, framing a face etched with age and sorrow. The stranger

2

was a woman, and she looked as though she could be anywhere between thirty and fifty years old. Her gnarled fingers were hooked into the straps of the backpack, and she continued to approach the chain across the entrance with careful, measured steps. Her feet were hidden by the long, ragged skirt she wore, its color long since faded to a neutral, dirty beige. She smiled at Wendy, and Wendy smiled back.

"Can you spare some change?" the woman asked, coming to a stop a few feet on the other side of the slim barrier. "I want to go up to the convenience store and get something to eat. Maybe a pack of cigarettes. Hey, have you got a cigarette on you?"

"No," Wendy said. "I'm sorry, I don't. I might have some change, though."

"Really?" she said, taking a step closer. She straightened up slightly. "Sure would be nice of you."

"Tough times?" Wendy asked. She opened her safety vest, unzipped her hoodie and reached into the pocket of her shirt.

"Terrible," the woman said softly. Her voice was suddenly soothing, and she licked her lips. She seemed taller. She eased herself closer.

"Are you going to the Cumberland Farms gas station?" Wendy asked conversationally.

"Yes," she murmured. She reached the gate and her hands extended from the ends of her sleeves.

The fingers, Wendy noticed, were exceptionally thin, the forefingers longer than the middles. And each finger was tipped with a long, dull gray nail, the edges of which looked wickedly sharp.

Wendy smiled at her, pulled her money out of her shirt pocket, and showed it to the woman.

"Thank you," the old woman whispered, her eyes locking onto Wendy. They were large and pale, lighter than the moon.

Wendy looked away, with some difficulty, and focused on her money. She unfolded the bills, revealed a small, clear plastic bag, and turned it upside down, emptying the contents onto the ground.

Thousands and thousands of grains of iodized salt fell to the cracked pavement.

3

The woman's eyes widened, and she let out a shriek of dismay.

She dropped to the road, her knees striking the pavement loudly, and she began to count the individual grains.

"Why?" she asked with a moan. "Why? *Why?!*"

"What's your name?" Wendy asked.

The woman didn't answer; she remained focused on the salt.

"What is your name?" Wendy demanded.

The woman snarled, looked up and spat, "Mary!"

"Mary," Wendy said, nodding. "Nice name. Mine's Wendy."

Mary ignored her, carefully making a pile of the grains she had already counted.

It was an exceptionally small pile.

While she focused on her task, Wendy reached back into her sweatshirt and freed her pistol. It was a small nine-millimeter automatic. Wendy whistled to herself, brought her fanny-pack around to the front, and she opened it. From its overstuffed depths, she removed a suppressor. With long practiced motions, she screwed the suppressor into the barrel of the automatic and chambered a round.

Mary glanced up at Wendy and snarled, "Bullets won't work. I'm no werewolf. I'll shred your flesh before I'm through with you."

"Yes," Wendy said. "I'm sure you'd like to."

She took careful aim at Mary's right knee and fired.

The pistol gave a small bark and the right knee, the entire joint, vanished. The specially cast, gold, hollow tipped round destroyed it.

Mary let out a shriek of rage, yet she continued to count.

She couldn't stop herself.

Wendy stepped over the chain and kicked the severed lower leg away. A foul, stinking black ichor leaked from the wound, but nothing more.

"It has been a while since you've eaten," Wendy said, walking around to the other side of her. "Guess the jogger who disappeared last month was your last meal?"

"Shut up!" Mary snapped as she continued to count.

4

Wendy shrugged, lined up a shot on Mary's left knee and pulled the trigger.

Mary let out a torrent of angry words, which sounded vaguely Gaelic, but still she couldn't turn away from the salt.

Cautiously, Wendy kicked the left leg away, glanced at the salt pile, which was diminishing rapidly, and brought her pistol up again. Her heart fluttered. She had come to the most dangerous part of the task.

A shot to the throat and even the banshee's compulsive need to count would be overridden by the desire to survive. Mary might not attack her, but the creature could certainly slip away into darkness.

Severing the arms would also free Mary of the compulsion to count, and, depending on how strong she was, she might be able to attack Wendy without her limbs.

But she hadn't been hunting Baobhan Sith banshees for thirty years to give up or shrink away.

The explosive-tipped rounds in the pistol gave her an edge, as did her skill with the weapon. So Wendy took the same chance she always did. She could only hope she was faster than Mary's instinct to survive.

Wendy was.

Four quick shots separated Mary's arms at the elbows and nearly severed her neck.

Mary fell back, her mouth working frantically in silent rage. A single artery kept her head attached to her body, and this, Wendy shot as well. Quickly, she took a plastic bag from her pack, shook it open and grabbed the banshee's head by the hair. The hate in Mary's eyes was powerful, and Wendy smiled at her as she dropped the head into the bag. She tied it off, set it down on the pavement, and went about the dirty process of dragging the various parts of Mary's body down the driveway.

She came to a worn and battered log cabin labeled, "OFFICE" in faded yellow letters. Wendy dropped Mary's forearms onto the ground and returned for the banshee's legs. When those had joined the arms, Wendy went back for the torso. By the time she had gotten it to the others, she was sweating and shaking her head at the stink coming off her clothes.

5

Finally, Wendy went back for Mary's head. She could see the banshee's lips working beneath the plastic. With a sigh, Wendy picked up the bag by its knot and kept it at arm's length. She didn't need Mary to bite through the bag.

And that's how hunters die, Wendy thought. *One moment of forgetfulness. A split second of stupidity.*

When Wendy got to the pile which remained of Mary's body, she set the banshee's head down to one side. She was an old creature from what Wendy could tell. A sense of power exuded from Mary, even dismembered as she was.

And Wendy felt better. The old ones traveled alone. They knew better than to hunt in groups. Too many people missing, and the local folk get concerned. It was best to snatch one or two. It made the Baobhan Sith harder to find.

Unless you know what to look for, Wendy thought. She had been tracking Mary's movements for nearly a year. The banshee had worked her way from upstate New York, down to the city, up into Connecticut, to the tip of Maine, and back down into New Hampshire. Almost a dozen dead. Runners, walkers, joggers. People who could conceivably go missing. Victims of unknown crimes.

Wendy straightened up, took her can of lighter fluid out of her pack and flipped it open.

Something cried. A low whining.

She stopped, the container poised above the remains. Wendy looked around and saw that the door to the office was ajar. Whatever it was cried again, and the sound came from the building.

Oh, Jesus, Wendy thought, putting the lighter fluid down on the ground. *Is there a kid in there?*

She pulled a fresh magazine out of the pack, ejected the one in the pistol and replaced it quickly. She chambered a round, took a firm grip on the weapon and advanced toward the structure.

The cries increased in volume, each plaintive sound pulling at her. Wendy steeled herself against the possibility of a bitten child. In all of her years hunting the undead, she had only had to put one young boy down. She still had nightmares about it.

Wendy took a deep breath, gently climbed up the stairs and pushed the door fully open with her left hand. Her flashlight flickered and cast strange shadows around the room. She smelled earth and death, age and sorrow. The room was barren of furniture, but in the corner was a pile of blankets, and from the worn fabric, she saw a small face peering at her. A little girl, dark haired and with exceptionally white skin.

Wendy lowered the pistol slightly, and then she saw the girl's eyes. Pale, exactly like Mary's. As Wendy went to bring the weapon back up, the girl hissed. The vicious, needle-shaped teeth of a Baobhan Sith glared from her mouth. Sharp, gray nails extended from the tips of the girls fingers.

Before Wendy could pull the trigger, something slammed into her, and she shot wildly into the ceiling. Wendy was sent spinning into the far wall. The girl launched herself out of the blankets, and a smaller child scrambled over Wendy. The disturbing clack of miniature hooves on the worn floorboards rang out, a harsh reminder of the lost humanity of the turned children.

The gun was quickly ripped from Wendy's hand and thrown across the room. Long fingernails latched onto her wrist, punching deep into her flesh and penetrating her veins. Even as she struggled to shake the child off, the girl landed on Wendy's chest. Her sternum cracked and ribs shattered.

She jerked Wendy's head back, drove her long nails into Wendy's throat. Wendy winced as dry lips attached themselves to the wounds on her throat, and the young banshee began to drink.

The instant loss of blood sapped Wendy of her strength, her efforts to free herself becoming no more potent than a fish flopping in the bottom of a canoe. The thrum of her own blood in her ears sank to a dull murmur, her heartbeat slowed.

Slowly, her consciousness faded, and Wendy was left with one terrible thought.

Dear God, they're not going to kill me...

* * *

The Doctor's Questions
By Eric Whittle

I can't open my eyes enough to see exactly what the room looks like. Only the outline of my legs, a bed, some tubes, and a cheap paper gown. My hand appears to have some kind of bracelet around it, most likely a hospital admittance bracelet; the kind with name and DOB. Wait. Then how did I end up in the hospital? Why hasn't my family been notified? Why can't I remember? Why do I feel so weak? I can feel my heartbeat all the way down to my feet. I'm panicking. No, I'm not, I'm fine - everything is fine. I'm in a hospital, I am safely admitted, and they are taking care of me. That's what hospitals are for.

If I had my wallet on me when I got here, then they must have my information on this bracelet I'm wearing. No need to over-react. My heartbeat slows at the thought. I can see a bit clearer. Maybe I can lift my arm and check if I can read it. It's taking a lot more effort than it normally would, even in my current state of fatigue. I hear a jingle as I raise it, then a sharp metallic pop as my wrist jerks to a sudden stop. I don't have to see clearly to know that I'm wearing a very different kind of bracelet. Steel cuffs, attached to the side rail of a hospital bed. Ones I have no recollection of getting in. This isn't treatment for an accident; this is detainment for an incident.

As the feeling of dread and impending doom roots itself, the sound of a door opening jolts me back to reality. Even though it seems as though I'm looking through grease-smeared glass instead of eyes, I can still make out the features of what can only be a doctor; a tall, old, white man with graying hair and a clipboard.

"Look who's awake," the Doctor says through a half-hearted grin while approaching my bed.

I don't respond. I feel like I can't. I might say something that would make my situation worse. I think he can see the look of dread on my face, because his grin turns to a rather loud, animated laugh.

"Why are you laughing? I don't understand," I manage to let out with a quivering tone.

"You do that every time! How could I not laugh?" the Doctor says as he scoots his rolling chair a foot away from the cuffed side of my bed. I can see a nametag now; *Dr. Tesion.*

"What do you mean 'every time'? I've never seen you before now, Dr. *tess-yawn*," I sneer.

"Yes, you have seen me, and you pronounce my name wrong every single time."

As he sits down, my vision starts to clear up enough to make out the finer details of his face, which are exactly as I expect; an old man with a large nose, wrinkled withering face, and a white lab coat.

"It's pronounced Dr. *tee-she-en*, not that it matters. You'll just call me doctor. You always do," he says. He starts flipping through pages on his clipboard while chuckling. Licking his finger each time he turns a page. He stops after a few flips, then squints at the paper. "Well, I won't sugar coat it. You messed yourself up pretty bad. Your vision is blurry, correct?"

"Yes."

"That's because you slammed into another vehicle on the I-15, and your head smashed into the windshield," he half-laughs, half-speaks his words. Why does he seem so giddy to tell me this? My feeling of dread mixes with seething anger. How can a medical doctor smile while delivering this kind of news?

"What the hell is wrong with you? Why are you laughing?"

He laughs even harder when I say that.

"Well Ryan, that's what we're going to figure out together," the Doctor says, his smile turning into a look of whimsical interest. "I noticed you have a lot of questions, but no sense of priority. Aren't you a bit more curious about why *I'm* here talking to you instead of the police?" he says, tapping the cuffed rail with his clipboard.

"Yes," I say. He may be inconsiderate, but he's right.

"Good. I've convinced the police that you need a different sort of attention than the type they want to give you. However, I can only keep them convinced if you do, too. I need one-hundred percent of your cooperation," he says, more serious now. "What I mean is, you need to stay calm and follow my

9

instructions. You do that, and things will turn out better than they have in the past," the Doctor says.

"I will only agree to that if you agree to clarify 'better than they have in the past'. If you're going to keep being a vague fortune teller, I'd rather talk to the police," I say.

"You can't fully understand what I meant by that until we figure it out together. Even so, I will tell you this, Ryan, if you don't accept the things that I say, whether you know what they mean or not, *you will not like the outcome*," the Doctor warns, almost as if to threaten.

I'm in no position to refuse. I don't even know what I did. I don't even know what hospital I'm at. If he's telling the truth about the police, then I should figure out what I did before making any decisions. This *Dr. Tesion* is the only one offering any answers. I have no choice but to go along.

"Alright, I'll cooperate. What do you need me to do?" I say.

"All I need you to do is answer questions, not ask them," he replies.

"That's physically impossible in my situation."

"It's difficult, I know. Just refrain from questions as much as possible. Before we do anything, your physical health needs to be addressed," he says, pointing to my head. "The blow to your head caused damage to the frontal and occipital lobes in your brain; the very front and very back areas. It got bounced around pretty good. As we mentioned briefly, that caused some vision issues; blurriness, and some other things. Look around, is anything abnormal?" he says, gesturing towards the entire room.

I look around. The blurriness seems to have completely gone away, but there's something else; something *wrong*. I scan the stationary objects around the room. Medical devices, tools and so forth. They look as if they are evaporating out of the corner of my vision. Then appearing all at once as soon as I look directly at them. This is concerning, confusing. Then I look at the Doctor.

I don't know how I could have missed it before, but it seems as though he is made out of plastic and rubber. His caricature of a face, with its many wrinkles and contours, looks like a wax carving. His eyes are the only things that seem to have any life in them, though it is stretched thin. This life is decaying and sorrowful. The kind you'd see in a soldier who has watched the last remnant of a soul leave their friends' eyes, time and time again. And in cruel irony, have taken that remnant from others' as well. As I keep looking at the Doctor's eyes, the rest of his face starts to evaporate like the room had done, moments ago.

Now, my vision is taken up completely by his eyes, which turn into two black abysses. I'm not sure if I can look away from them, or if time is distorted and I've been here for an eternity. I feel as though all of the guilt and sadness in the world have been poured into these eyes. Poured into me. I can see my reflection in those black pits, but not a reflection of my face or body - a reflection of me, of who I am. These voids are hell. These voids are me.

I hear a voice screaming, and then whimpering, over and over again. It's getting louder. Time has gained hold again, the unending black is evaporating. I see eyes. They're mine. No, they're the Doctor's. I can see his face now, he's standing over me. The screaming is deafening now. I want it to stop. Over the screaming, I can hear the sound of metal and glass crunching together, screeching. The sounds mix together, and intertwine. I realize, suddenly, that the screaming is coming from my own mouth. I try for a while to silence myself, and eventually manage to lower the scream to quiet weeping.

I regain regular sight. I look down at my cuffed wrist. The skin is eviscerated. My gown is covered in blood and bits of flesh, bone fragments and all other manner of viscera. I gasp in disgust, as if I were looking at a butchered animal instead of my own arm. The pain sets in slowly, then all at once. My wrist feels like it's being bashed by rocks while a blowtorch scorches any remaining nerves that may have been spared. The agony is matched by the volume of my screams. They reverberate into my ears as I close my eyes, and then fade away as I open them. When I do, I see the Doctor.

"Look around. Is anything abnormal?" I hear the doctor say.

I'm staring at him. The pain is gone. I look at my wrist, there is no blood. I would scream, but I continue to stare at the Doctor, instead. I start to fall into the abyss again.

"No!" I yell, closing my eyes and turning away.

"There we go. That was much quicker than usual," the Doctor says.

"What does that even mean? What is this, what kind of Doctor are you?" I ask, frantically.

"No questions, remember?" he reiterates.

"No, you are going to answer *my* questions, now!" I shout, starting to reach towards the Doctor, unsure of what I'd do if I actually grab hold of him.

The doctor backs away, quickly and calmly. As I yell insults and threats at him, he sits and patiently waits. I finally calm down. I'm breathing hard, I can feel every negative emotion in the spectrum; I don't care why I'm here. I don't care who this 'Doctor' is anymore. I want this to end. I don't understand. The Doctor lets out a loud sigh then begins to speak.

"Your head injury has made you ..."

"No. This is not the result of some head injury. doctor. This is your doing. Everything is normal - as normal as it can get in my situation, until you start to ask your questions. You have done no tests on me. You have provided me with no evidence that this isn't an elaborate kidnap and torture!" I protest.

"Yes, I have Ryan. More times than I'd like to admit, or that you'd remember," he says all in one breath, tiredly.

"And I'm supposed to take your word for it? I'm supposed to accept what you're putting me through because you have a nametag? I don't care how many times you've done the tests, even if I don't remember. *Do them again,*" I yell.

The doctor is laughing again, harder than before. He's close to tears.

"Oh, this is funny again? Why? Because I've ..."

"Yes, you've said this all before Ryan! I've heard your insane ramblings about the abyss, your ceaseless weeping and the screams - all of it! I know about the disappearing objects. Losing your sense of time comes right before the hallucinations of near dismemberment, right?" he says, shaking his head.

"I could tell you what happens next, but every time I do, I lose you and we go right back to square one. I know I'm making you angry, I have to. It's the only way to keep you going. The sooner you understand that, the sooner you can make sense of this and someday come out of it," the Doctor proclaims, putting his hands in the air, as to suggest 'it's that easy'.

The Doctor continues, "As for your claims of me holding you hostage, look," he gets up, and opens the door. "Nurse!" he yells. Some moments later, a very large male nurse in blue scrubs walks into the room. "Yes doctor?" As the man says this, the Doctor points at me. The nurse starts to let out a slight chuckle and says, "Hostage or conspiracy?"

"Hostage," the Doctor answers. He gestures for the nurse to leave, then closes the door.

My feeling of powerlessness and stupidity doubles as the Doctor takes his seat, flips to a page on his clipboard, then stares at me.

"I get it now, I understand," I say, solemnly. "I'm insane, and you have been trying to help me."

"*Yes*, Ryan, but we wouldn't call it insanity," he responds with genuine concern.

"Okay. If I don't accept that fact I slip back again, right?" I ask.

"Right again. Unfortunately, that is the case," he says.

"Could you, at least, tell me how long this has been going on?"

"Another problem with treating you is that I can't even tell you how long I've been treating you without another relapse. But I'll put it this way, when you first got here, you remembered your family. Do you still remember them?" he asks.

I spent so much time being combative that I couldn't think of something so fundamental.

"I don't . . . I don't remember them," I say.

I have to accept this, I can't let my overwhelming sadness take hold. The Doctor is right, he has to be. How else would he know all of this?

"Are you ready for the rest of the questions? The first one is always the hardest. You're past it now. There are a few easy questions, then the last one, which we've never been able to get past," he says.

"Yes I'm ready," I say as confidently as I can.

The Doctor lets out a long sigh of relief.

"When you were in your 'abyss', do you remember anything about a crash?" he asks.

"I heard metal scraping, glass breaking, and screams. But I don't remember seeing anything," I say.

"Who did the screams belong to Ryan?" he asks.

"Me, but at the same time they didn't belong to me. It's hard to explain," I reply.

"Who did they belong to, if you had to guess?" he asks.

"If I collided with another vehicle, it must have been the people I hit," I say. I can taste something pungent in my mouth. It leaves as quickly as it comes.

"What road were you driving on Ryan?" the Doctor asks.

"Interstate 15, from Barstow to Las Vegas," I respond immediately.

"Good, Ryan. You're doing very well. So you started you trip in Barstow. What's in Barstow?" the Doctor asks as he shifts forward in his seat.

"My family is there. My wife and children."

The taste comes back to my mouth, stronger now. It tastes like hard liquor mixed with charcoal.

"Why did you leave them?" he asks.

"The police were called," tears fill my vision and my voice begins to crack.

"Called by whom?" he asks.

"I don't know. I was fighting with my wife. She said I'm a useless drunk, that I'm not good for the children," I can barely speak through my sobbing. I can see my kids through the window above the kitchen sink, Kayla and Cameron. Kayla is nine, Cameron is twelve. They're playing outside. They look so happy. I can see my wife, Amy, yelling at me in the kitchen. I can't hear her, though.

"We had to make them go outside. She didn't want the kids to hear," I speak as if driven by a motor.

"Why were you fighting?" the Doctor asks.

"I had gone over to her house drunk again, I don't know why. I wanted to see the kids. I couldn't think straight. I just wanted to see my kids."

"At what point did it get out of hand?" the Doctor asks, his voice sounding distant. I can't see the doctor or the hospital bed anymore. I'm standing in my house in Barstow, drunk, having a screaming match with my wife. I can hear her clearly now.

Seven years. Seven friggin' years Ryan, and not one day can you just show up sober, can you? Your kids haven't seen their father since they were babies. You're lucky I don't call the police! You know what? If you don't leave right now, I will call the police.

She reaches for her phone; I put it in the garbage disposal and turn it on. She starts to run towards the door, I block her from getting out. She runs into her bedroom. She thinks I am going to hit her. I would never hit her, but she would always cower like I was going to. She gets to the bedroom before I do. I try to grab the handle, but my hand slips through the door as she slams it on my wrist. I can't feel the pain but I know it's there. I push through the doorway into the bedroom; she still thinks I am going to hit her. I just want to talk. I don't know why I keep going. I don't know why I think she would want to talk to me. I just want her to let me see my kids. She tries to grab my gun that I had left in the dresser drawer when she kicked me out, but I get to it first. I am not pointing it at her; I'm just keeping it away from her. She starts to scream at me again.

Look at you Ryan! Big man! You've got a gun now! You wouldn't pull that trigger. You couldn't. You're a useless drunk just like your Father. His death got you sober for what - a day?

15

Tears are streaming down my face as I put the gun in my mouth. I can hear my daughters outside playing. I'll have peace, finally.

That's just like you isn't it, get all this way just to seek more attention. Well, congratulations Ryan. We're all proud of you.

She keeps talking for a moment or two, I'm not listening. I take the gun out of my mouth, and shoot her. In the chest, I think. I don't look when I pull the trigger, I don't want to see it. I drop the gun and run out to the front lawn where my kids are playing. They ask what the loud sound was. I say it was their mom turning on a movie, and that she'd let us go on a trip while she watched it. I grab a bottle of Vodka from under the sink, and then we drive down Interstate 15. I think the traffic lane headed in the other direction is a passing lane. My daughters are playing in the back, I am so happy. They keep playing, even as I drive the car into oncoming traffic. Screams. Crunching metal. Breaking glass. A dark abyss.

I can hear The Doctor's voice again.

"Last question Ryan. What is this *'hospital'*?"

As the feeling of dread and impending doom roots itself, the sound of a door opening jolts me back to reality. Even though it seems as though I'm looking through grease-smeared glass instead of eyes, I can still make out the features of what can only be a doctor; a tall, old, white man with graying hair and a clipboard.

* * *

Urbex
By David Longhorn

It's raining, leaving the roads and sidewalks slick in the glow of streetlights. A good night, I feel. Sometimes you just know when things will run smoothly. Of course, sometimes your instincts are wrong. It's always worth bearing that in mind.

I arrive at the pub a few minutes early to check out the place and make sure there's a quiet corner. I park the van out of sight of the main road, lock it, look around to see if I'm being watched. Nothing's obviously wrong, so I go inside. It's quiet, almost empty, in fact, a typical midweek lull unenlivened by quiz or karaoke. It's one reason why I chose the place as a rendezvous. I nod to the barmaid, she pours me a pint of my usual tipple, and as she works the pump, we exchange a few platitudes about the weather, traffic, and the abysmal performance of the local soccer team.

She jerks her head, says, "They're in the back room."

I thank her and go through.

There are four 'urban explorers' tonight, three under thirty, one much older, all wearing outdoor gear, which is ironic. They're chatting away, none too quietly, and I resist the temptation to shush them. First, establish authority. I put my pint down and stand over them. Silence falls. I introduce myself, not using my real name, of course. They have to, though. That's part of the deal. I've got to check out clients beforehand. You can't be too careful when you're operating in a legal gray area. Thanks to careful research I can put names to faces.

The twenty-somethings are Keith and Kim, very much a couple, all snuggly on the leather bench, sharing smiles, touches, a bit of mild shoving. Love's young dream. I try to be cynical, but I miss that sort of warmth, human contact, finishing one another's sentences, all the stuff that advertising execs love. But time brings its compensations.

The old guy is Bruce, a know-it-all, fancies himself an expert. He might be a problem. Like many a bore he has no idea how tedious his endless monologues on technical matters

17

are. He is the sort who turns up on comment threads and sets everyone right, to his own satisfaction. Still, he is a smallish, weedy guy, so at least he can't throw his weight around.

Josh is the youngster of the group, late teens or early twenties, black-clad, intense, fancy sleeve tattoo. Judging by his online activity he is a bit of crank, into crypto-zoology, UFOs, conspiracy theories, God knows what else. But you get all sorts in this game. It's not what you call regular tourism.

Having introduced myself, I pull up a stool and sit down.

"Right, let's just run over the ground rules one more time," I say.

Josh rolls his eyes while Keith-Kim giggle, shove each other. Bruce is looking at me intensely. He has a low blink-rate.

"Firstly, we stick together. Nobody goes off alone, nobody lags behind. If anyone breaks that rule, I turn back and leave the way we came in. Is that clear?"

Bruce clears his throat. Christ, here we go.

"I understand that we'll be visiting an area you are already familiar with? Therefore you could have provided us with a chart of the tunnels—"

I interrupt him, rudely. It's the only way, sometimes.

"I'm the one who's taking the risks, here. I don't just give out information to anyone who can then stick it on a website, or set up a rival business. And this is a business, which reminds me, fifty pounds each. In advance."

They hand over the money with varying degrees of grace. Keith-Kim are obviously young professionals more used to paying with plastic; their notes have that fresh from the ATM look. Bruce pays up under protest, as I expected. Josh produces some well-worn bills that he might have pinched from his mother's purse. Well, at least he's not spending it on drugs.

"Okay," I say, pocketing the dosh. "Second ground rule, you leave your phones in my van."

Protests, of course. I raise a hand for quiet.

"They don't work underground except when you're near a vent or drain or whatever, and sending any kind of signal is a bad idea. The local cops have become much more aware of urbexing lately and sometimes they can pinpoint a cellphone signal. It's unlikely, but not impossible."

"But we wanted to make a video!" protests Kim. "I mean, people won't believe we went down there otherwise!"

She's sweet; they both are really, the sort of people who can't help feeling bad about disappointing.

"You can borrow this, if you like," I say, and produce a small digital camera. "The SD memory card is included in the price. I've got more in the van. All part of the service."

Mollified, Keith-Kim start to examine the camera, film each other goofing around.

"Christ, I think I'm getting diabetes," mutters Josh.

"Third rule," I say. "No matter what happens, you do what I tell you. I know this underground space, you don't. The whole of this area is honeycombed with old coal mines, plus Victorian sewers and drains, and World War Two bomb shelters. They all interconnect, and a lot of them are poorly-maintained and ready to collapse. So if I say run, you run. If I say stand absolutely still, you make like statues. Understood?"

"Yes, sir!" says Kim, giving a mock salute.

"Right, we might as well drink up and then get moving," I say. But now Josh is waving his phone in front of me.

"I want to know if this is where we're going," he asks.

There's a video running on the phone, and I recognize it at once. I hear tiny screams from the speaker, vague forms thrash around. A face, inhumanly pale with huge black eyes, appears briefly in close-up. A greenish light reflects from dank tunnel walls.

"Ooh, we saw that one, too!" exclaims Kim.

Bruce snorts.

"I've seen it. Obviously fake," he says. "Amateurish nonsense! Especially the ending. Not even decent CGI, more like old-style green screen."

"Look," I say, before they can start bickering, "I've seen that clip and, whatever people are saying, it could have been made anywhere. Yes, they seem to have British accents judging by their cries for help – which seem a bit overdone by the way. But there are tunnels like that all over the country. One

Victorian drain looks much like another. And, as Bruce says, the whole thing screams fake."

Josh has frozen the video, holds up the phone. A humanoid thing, hairless, with huge clawed hands, is sinking its teeth into the neck of a half-naked man. The victim looks comically frightened, staring at the camera with a look that says *I can't believe this is happening!*

"That's pretty good work, if it is fakery," says Josh. "The makeup, prosthesis, all of that stuff looks professional to me. But nobody's taken credit for it. There's no point in making a horror film, even a five minute one, and not using it to get some kudos, advance your career, is there?"

Keith-Kim look worried, now, but Bruce comes to the rescue with another snort, his gray nostril-hairs quivering with contempt.

"They have to wait for it to go viral, get a certain number of hits, before they announce it's a hoax, don't they? Even I know that."

"It's been out there for weeks," protests Josh. "It's got nearly half a million hits!"

Five minutes of desultory argument follows, then we are all finished with our drinks and ready to go. I take them out to the van and dish out their respective kits. Not just the cheap cameras but also hard hats with lamps.

"Safety first," I tell them. "Though I don't think they provide protection from underground cannibal monsters."

Josh scowls, but takes his kit with the rest. The phones are deposited in the van, and we are then good to go. It's a short walk up the road to the old Civil Defense Headquarters, a 1940s bunker converted for Cold War usage and decommissioned at the turn of the century. The place is set well back from the road, but I caution them not to put their hard hats on until we are inside. There's a hole in the fence I covered with some old junk, easy to crawl through. Then we nip round the side of the building to a door that I locked with my own padlock.

"Hats on, but wait until we're inside before switching on your lights," I tell them.

The old bunker is a series of concrete and steel boxes. There's nothing much of interest apart from a few tattered maps on the walls, filing cabinets long since gutted, and small piles of canned food. Relics of a conflict that never happened. We move quickly through and down, taking the stairs to the basement, then the sub-basement. Bruce is right behind me, giving a running commentary on NATO, nukes, Cuban Missile Crisis, the works. Keith-Kim are pissing off Bruce in their silly, gentle way while Josh is silent, tagging along at the back. He's still brooding on the video, I guess.

We reach the end of the sub-basement room where the wall has collapsed.

"This is due to subsidence in old mine-workings," I tell them. "As such, it's risky to go through. I'm giving you this warning now so nobody can claim I misled you later. Should anything happen."

"Abandon all hope, ye who enter here!" says Keith.

It's all a big giggle to some people.

"Just so we're clear," I say, and lead them into the Victorian storm drains.

They are impressed. Bruce talks about 'a great achievement of the Industrial Revolution' and for once I have to agree with him. Keith-Kim make assorted 'wow' noises and film in all directions, but mostly end up focusing on one another. Josh is still a surly little bugger, but his money is as good as anyone's.

"Right, we go downhill, under the city," I say. "Stick close, if you twist your ankle or your light goes out, anything like that, give a yell. Don't get strung out, don't go into any side passages, don't dawdle. We stay together, understood? It's the only safe way."

"It doesn't seem that dangerous," observes Kim.

"There are rats down here," I point out, and as I expected, this pretty much glues her to Keith's side for the rest of the expedition.

The next ten minutes or so are spent sloshing through rainwater that inevitably gets in through dozens of faults and cracks. At one point, there's a slight vibration and a distant rumble. I tell them that we are slap-bang underneath the main coastal railroad line. Bruce looks skeptical at this but, for a mercy, says nothing.

"It's getting a bit warmer, how's that happen?" asks Keith.

"Deeper you get, the warmer it gets," chips in Bruce. "Basic geophysics, I think you'll find."

"That's when you go really deep," objects Keith. "I mean, we're talking miles down, nearer the earth's what-you-call-it, magma?"

"We're quite deep," I say. "But remember, there's also some carbon dioxide build up down here. It's heavier than air."

That quiets them for a while, and then we arrive at the end of the main drain. There's a big iron grille that looks out onto an underground river, flowing through a huge culvert to the sea about two miles east.

"Is that it?" asks Josh, incredulous.

"The end of the line," I say.

They crowd forward to look through the grille, their lamps playing on the rusted iron bars.

"Wow, it's spooky!" says Kim, shoving her camera through to film the culvert.

Josh is looking around at the walls of the drain, his lamp throwing glistening circles of blue-white light over the curved brickwork.

I walk back up the drain until I'm about fifteen feet away, then turn and look back. Josh looks at me, his lamp blinding.

"What's wrong?" he asks.

"Nothing," I say.

I take out my phone and start filming.

"Hey!" Josh shouts, "You said we couldn't—"

Then his expression changes as it starts to dawn on him, too late. Behind him the iron grille vanishes in a greenish glow. Kim screams, pulls her arm back to reveal a smoking stump where her hand was.

That's another camera gone. Shit.

"Jesus Christ!"

Bruce is backing off quickly for an old guy, but not fast enough. The first of the visitors leaps out of the portal and wraps its arms and legs around him, plunges fangs into his neck. Almost a shot-for-shot remake of the last video, in fact. I imagine Bruce is stringy old meat but perhaps all the more flavorsome for that. The next one takes down Keith, who is trying to wrap a tourniquet around Kim's arm. Nice young couple, but slow when it counts.

Josh is faster and nearly makes it to me before another visitor tackles him, starts to drag him back towards the portal. He screams. Well, who wouldn't? Another visitor leaps, and the two start to tear at his legs and buttocks, too hungry to wait. The iron smell of blood is heavy, now, and it does indeed seem warm down here.

It's all over in less than three minutes.

When the visitors are finished they reward me with life, as they have done regularly since they spared me that first time, back when we were fixing the storm drain before the war. The first Great War, that is. I've learned a lot since then, of course, but not much about them. I still don't know what they are, or where they come from, only what they need. Maybe one day they'll kill me, or come through in force and kill everyone.

Or perhaps they'll simply stop coming, and I'll grow old and die like everyone else.

Until then, we have a deal.

With judicious editing the video will be at most ninety seconds, maybe less. The trick is to make it look cheap and contrived, first-year film studies stuff at best. Too real and questions may be asked in high places. Too little detail and nobody will be interested. There's an art to making it viral and it's a pain, trying to get it right. But when I think of how hard it used to be to lure people down here, I can only give thanks for the miracles of modern technology.

* * *

Museum Quality
By Ron Ripley

Devin could hardly contain his excitement.

He hurried into his dining room, put the package down on the table and turned the chandelier on. Brilliant, white light spilled over the room and illuminated his newest purchase.

His hands shook as he untied the twine used to keep the brown paper to the box. As the rough cord fell to the table top, the wrapper sprang away. Devin pushed the rest of it down and removed the thin, silver cardboard container.

He sat down, inserted his thumbnail between the top of the box and the edge, then neatly severed the scotch tape which had kept the container sealed. From within, he pulled out the bill of sale and a piece of heavy weight paper. Each corner of the curious bit of parchment had been folded in to the center, where they met and were held in place by a thick circle of dark green wax. The image of a scarab could be clearly seen in the sealing wax.

Devin broke the seal and opened the letter. Upon the paper were five sentences.

The first was written in Egyptian hieroglyphs, the second looked to be Greek, the third was undeniably Latin, the fourth was Arabic, and the fifth was, more than likely, Hebrew.

And Devin could read absolutely none of it.

"*You do, I trust, have access to the internet?*" the dealer had asked him.

Devin did have access, of course, and he said as much.

"*There is a warning here, and a precaution to take,*" the dealer had said. "*You must translate and read it for yourself. It cannot be told. Do you understand?*"

"*Yes,*" Devin had answered. "*I understand. I understand completely.*"

It was only upon his agreement to research the warning that the man had sold him the item.

For what was in the box, though, Devin would have promised the strange little antiques dealer anything he asked for.

Devin set the paper down on the table, wiped his hands absently on his pants and removed his newest piece. A beautiful, dark wood case. Museum glass had been expertly fitted between the wooden framework and stood upon a slightly wider base of the same colored wood.

Within the nearly one-foot square case was the true prize, however.

It was a diorama of three large beetles and a massive, long legged spider Devin had never seen before.

The taxidermist who had built the piece had been a master of his art. Each beetle was arranged artfully upon a trio of branches, dried grass glued to the wooden base. Dirt had been attached to the bottom as well, and several large pieces of dried fungal growth had been secured to the branches.

The three beetles were of different sizes. The first, and located the highest in the display, was a deep purple, almost black color. No larger than a silver dollar. The second, frozen in the act of leaving one branch for another, was slightly larger, with a dark green color which shimmered in the light. The last, and by far the largest of the beetles, stood in the center. It looked as though it were an Egyptian scarab, except it was a brilliant, powerful gold. Beneath the branches, peeking out from the shadows, was the spider.

Dark gray in color, with exceptionally long legs, the spider's eight eyes caught the light through the museum glass and glowed.

The antique dealer in Milford had asked for a high price, nearly three hundred, but it had been worth it.

Devin knew he had to have it as soon as he had set his eyes upon it.

For several minutes, he sat at the table and stared at it, smiling softly to himself. Finally, with a happy sigh, he stood up, gathered the paper wrapping and cardboard box into his arms and brought them to the recycling bin. He dropped them in, whistled a bit of Brahms to himself, and went about preparing himself a cup of tea.

As the water slowly came to a boil, he went to his phone, saw there was a call from his ex-wife, and ignored the message.

He knew he was late with the alimony.

He would mail the check out in the morning.

Devin kept an ear open for the kettle as he went around the apartment, drew the shades and inspected the maid's work. She had done an excellent job, as always, but his taxidermy collection always needed his close attention.

Other maids had failed in the past to care for his pieces the way they should be.

Janet was quite adept at her work, which was why he had retained her services for so long.

With his daily inspection finished, he returned to the kitchen as the water came to a boil. After a few moments, he had his mint tea prepared, and he sat down at the table.

Delicate tendrils of steam curled up from the surface of the liquid, and Devin looked lovingly at the beetles.

He had added many beautiful pieces to his collection over the years, but the display before him was absolutely stunning. He was enamored with the scarab, and could see why the ancient Egyptians had worshiped it.

The magnificent, almost regal way it perched upon its branch, spoke volumes about the taxidermist. The man had taken a tremendous amount of care with the placement of the insect, and Devin honestly didn't believe he could tire of looking at it.

Pleased with his newest acquisition, Devin sighed and drank his tea. When he finished it, he stifled a yawn, took the cup to the sink and rinsed it before he set it down. He returned to the table, picked up the strange letter and the diorama, and then carried them with him into his study. He placed the display on the mantle above the fireplace, turned on the gas flames, and retreated to his leather armchair.

He held up the letter and examined it again.

Should I? he asked himself, glancing over at his laptop.

With a groan, Devin forced himself out of the comfort of the chair and over to the computer. He continued to stand as he turned the laptop on. He brought up Google, found a good translating site and typed in the Latin sentence.

Cursed and bound, the translation read. *Touch not the Scarab, lest ye be touched. Life from your life, an evil awakened.*

Frowning, Devin straightened up. He looked at the Latin, made certain he had typed it in correctly, and saw that he had.

Curious little warning, Devin thought. He shut the laptop down and carried the letter back to the chair. He put the parchment down on the worn leather of the arm, hesitated, then went back to the display.

A curse! What absolute nonsense, he thought. A strong desire to feel the carapace beneath his skin filled him. Licking his lips excitedly, Devin cautiously lifted the top of the case off. A teasing hint of an exotic, unnamable perfume caressed his nose and he smiled.

Of course I can touch it, he thought, grinning. *It's mine.*

Devin reached in and felt the smooth body of the scarab. The sensation was sensual, titillating in a way he had never experienced with an item in his collection. Devin chuckled happily, withdrew his hand and replaced the top of the case.

Whistling to himself, Devin returned to the armchair, sank into it and settled back, making himself comfortable.

For a moment, he considered a celebratory brandy, but he was tired enough. Too early in the evening for liquor and he would never make it to watch the newest episode of *Sherlock* on PBS. A glance at the clock on his desk showed it was almost six.

A short nap, Devin thought, yawning again, *and then a light dinner. I can have my brandy later as I watch Holmes and Watson.*

He closed his eyes, settled into his chair and slipped his shoes off. He wriggled his toes through his socks and into the thick carpet. He smiled as he thought of his newest purchase.

The gas flames made their curious, soft popping sounds. From the kitchen, the hum of the refrigerator could be heard. Somewhere, out in the parking lot of his building, a car started, the engine loud.

All of the familiar noises served as a lullaby, and Devin easily drifted off to sleep.

A sharp crack sounded and snapped Devin back to consciousness.

He straightened up in the chair, accidentally knocked the letter onto the floor, rubbed his eyes and looked around the room.

According to the clock, it was a little after nine, and the darkness beyond the study's solitary window confirmed it.

The room was lit solely by the light of the fire. Devin reached out to the floor lamp, found the pull string and tugged at it.

He winced at the suddenness of the bulb's light, and it took him a moment to see clearly. Everything in the room was in sharp focus, and he quickly saw what had made the crack.

The front pane of glass on his beetle diorama had broken, the upper right corner of it laying on the carpet. It glinted in the light of the floor lamp, and Devin wondered how the roughly triangular piece could have fallen out, let alone break.

He stood up, walked over to the glass and picked it up.

It was curiously warm in his hands.

He put the segment on the mantle beside the diorama and smelled a sweet, delicate aroma. He looked in at the beetles.

Devin straightened up.

Where is it? he asked himself, staring at the display. *Where is it?*

The scarab was missing.

Gone.

Vanished from the branch.

Devin twisted around and looked at the other specimens in the study. Birds and small rodents. The upper portion of a black bear.

How the hell could the scarab have disappeared anyway? he thought.

He shook his head and forced himself to breathe deeply. With an effort, he brought his racing mind under control and carefully began searching the room. He didn't worry about any rational explanation as to *why* the glass might have broken, or *how* a long dead beetle could have gotten out.

Devin focused on the important thing.

Finding it.

He could always have the glass repaired, but it would be a moot point if he didn't have the beetle.

He looked down at the floor in front of the fire.

If the glass was there, the scarab should be close by, he thought.

Devin got down on his hands and knees. He crawled carefully, wary of any small shards of glass while he peered around for the beetle. After several minutes of searching, he caught sight of it.

The scarab was clinging to the underside of Devin's chair.

One of the insect's forelegs moved slowly, gently pulling at the thin strands of the black fabric beneath the seat.

Without getting to his feet, Devin moved forward, keeping his eyes locked on the escapee. He reached out, gently took hold of the scarab and carefully pulled it out from beneath the chair. The insect scuttled around the inside of his hand, its legs disgustingly warm.

"How," Devin started to say, but he stopped. Something brushed the back of his neck, and he felt sudden sharp pain.

Before he could swear, his arms and legs went stiff, he lost his balance, and he toppled over onto his left. By the time he struck the floor, he couldn't feel anything. His thoughts were muddy, and the effort to think was painful.

From where he lay on his side, he could still see the scarab. He watched as it turned around and seemed to focus its attention on him.

Then, from the corner of his eye, Devin saw a shape move.

Dark gray. Long legs. Quick, alien movements. The spider from the diorama.

It appeared from a shadow, carrying with it a large, pale egg sack made of finely woven silk.

And even through the curious haze in his mind, Devin realized two things.

First, it was the spider that had bitten him.

Second, the spider was not an 'it,' but rather a 'she.'

The scarab climbed down from the chair and joined the spider, taking the egg sack from her. The two creatures stood beside each other, and a moment later. The other two beetles from the diorama appeared. They took up positions on the egg, and the three beetles rolled it towards Devin.

The spider danced forward, picking her way delicately towards him with all of the grace of an insane ballerina.

Part of him desperately wanted to pull away, to get as far as possible from the arachnid.

But he couldn't.

Her venom had stilled his muscles, and when she reached him, she stretched out a foreleg gracefully. The sharp hairs on it caressed his cheek, and when he neither flinched nor screamed, she darted forward.

The beetles rolled the egg towards him while the female spider wove a web. She lay the anchor strand under his chin, and soon she raced back and forth across his face. Inwardly, he screamed, furious and terrified at the same time. He tried to pull away. Thin, powerful lines of silk were lain across his eyes, the lids open.

The beetles disappeared from his line of sight, and then he felt them. Legs working together up his neck, onto his cheek. They pushed the egg sack ever before them. With great care, they pried open his mouth and tucked the egg between lip and gum.

As the beetles backed away, the spider rushed across his face. She pulled his lips closed and sealed them shut with silk.

From where he lay on the floor, Devin could see the letter the antiques dealer had pressed upon him. He could see the light glow in the dark green of the wax seal, fragments of the various languages written in powerful, broad strokes.

What does it say? he thought desperately.

Then against the sensitive skin of his mouth, Devin felt the smooth surface of the egg sack and numbly wondered when the spiderlings would hatch.

* * *

Tell Me Your Name
By A.I. Nasser

"Tell me your name."

30

The woman sitting across from me smiled sweetly, welcoming even, her hands expertly shuffling the cards in her hand as she kept her eyes locked on mine. Despite my discomfort, I smiled back, trying to hide how out of place I felt in the dim, cramped up room. I had just gotten into my seat, although I knew she had taken an interest in me the moment I had walked in.

"Mustafa," I replied, nodding at the others sitting around the table. There were five us, including the pretty brunette, each hidden in the shadows of their own presence. I searched for any familiar faces, hoping to find someone I had met at earlier games, but failed to recognize any except for the man who had invited us. He was sitting in the seat next to mine, looking at me through tinted glasses that hid his eyes. His smile, though, said it all: We're going to eat you alive.

"Such a beautiful name," the woman said. "I'm Rhea. You'll get to know the rest in time."

I smiled sheepishly and stole a quick look back at my friend. Tamer was sitting on a couch in a more illuminated part of the room, surrounded by guests I could only assume were the other players' plus ones. He gave me a double thumbs up and smiled widely.

"I presume you know the rules?"

I did.

I had started playing *Kamera* a few years back, having been introduced to it by my doorman one night when the lights had gone out and I was too tired to walk up thirteen flights of stairs. Ever since the revolution, the power outages had become a frequent occurrence in Cairo, and it was customary for the electricity to 'take a break' for a few hours every day. That night I had come home late, my manager having had decided that eight pm was a little too early to stop working.

I remember contemplating whether or not to just stay in the car when my doorman had waved me over, a deck of cards in his hand, and asked if I were interested in learning a new game. I was a sucker for card games, once even reprimanded for gambling on university campus, and had been drawn in almost immediately.

"We play with a single queen," Rhea was saying, giving me a wink.

"It's the only way I know," I replied, my comment awarded with a sharp laugh from Glasses.

Kamera was basically poker, or at least the version of which you learned to play with your high school friends. The only difference was that the deck had one queen, a trump card that made you an instant winner no matter what suits the other players had in their hands. Other than that, it was basically about how well you could bluff, and I was good at that.

"Very well, let's begin."

I lost track of time quickly, engrossed in the game, studying the faces of my opponents as best as I could. I was doing well for the first few hands, keeping up with the best, quickly retiring two of the players who got up with huffs and scowls, retreating to the couches before leaving completely. A few hands later, and there were only three of us left at the table.

"The boy is lucky," Glasses said, the smile on his face now gone completely. I could tell he was secretly waiting for me to drop dead, and I smiled at the notion that I had gotten under his skin.

"Oh, I would say he's a lot more than that," Rhea cooed, eyeing me closely. Throughout the game, I had been the focus of her attention, noticing her stare at me from the corner of my eye as I played, bluffed, wagered, and folded. She was trying to read me, and I hoped I was giving her a hard time at that.

"Just deal the damn cards, Rhea," Glasses hissed.

She winked at me again, her slender fingers dancing in the air as she shuffled and dealt. I picked up my cards and fought the urge to laugh when I saw the queen amongst the rest. I kept my cool, looking over at Rhea and feeling very uncomfortable as she smiled at me, her cards untouched. Glasses made the first bet, and we both raised.

It went on like this for what I could only guess was an hour before Glasses slapped his cards down and got up in rage, heading straight for Rhea. "You're cheating, you whore!" he accused her, his face red with anger, his fists curled. Just before he could reach her, two men grabbed him by the arms and pulled him back. Rhea was shuffling the cards again, looking straight at me with that smile of hers and ignoring her attacker.

"You're being rude in front of our guest," she said calmly.

"Screw him!" Glasses blurted out. "And screw you, too, Rhea!"

She turned to look at him, her face almost serene, in complete control. "Are you withdrawing?"

"Damn right I'm withdrawing," Glasses shot back, pulling away from the guards and picking up the remainder of his chips. "Enjoy your new pet!" I met his stare just before he threw a few chips onto my own pile. "You're going to need those," he spat, and then turned and left the room.

My eyes followed him out, and quickly looked over at Tamer, the only guest left, as he shrugged and shook his head in bewilderment. When I turned around, Rhea gave me a quick wink and shuffled again.

"I assume you're still in," she said, matter-of-factly.

"Of course," I replied.

"Good," she cooed. "It would be a shame to lose a good player on his first day."

I watched her hands swiftly shuffle the cards, trying my best to make out if there were any truth to Glasses' accusations, but she was too fast. Suddenly, five cards were delivered to me, and the hostess watched closely as I picked them up and inspected them.

"You're a hard player to read," she said as I studied my royal flush.

"I try," I commented, again disturbed by the fact that she hadn't picked up her cards yet. I had a feeling that maybe Glasses was right. Why else would she not look at her hand unless she already knew what she had?

"Does my confidence disturb you?"

"Of course not," I lied, faking a smile. "I'm just new to the violence."

Rhea smiled, lifted the edges of her cards, and then looked up at me again. Raising one eyebrow, she pushed in her first bet.

33

I met hers and raised.

"No trades?"

"I'm comfortable with what I have."

She nodded and traded all five of her cards, briefly looking at her new hand. She pushed in more chips.

"I'll see you and raise," I said confidently.

"Let's make this a little more interesting," Rhea replied, all smiles, and threw in all her chips.

"I don't have that much," I said, looking over my shoulder and signaling for Tamer. "Will cash do for now?"

"I don't want your money," Rhea said. "How about you just throw in your name on top of those?"

I frowned, the idea a little foreign to me. "My name?"

"Your name," Rhea confirmed.

"You don't want money?" I was still confused. "How is my name of any value?"

"Oh, it is, sweetheart," Rhea smiled. "More than you think."

"Your loss," I said.

I threw down my cards and showed her my hand, smiling. Rhea inspected the cards only for a moment before turning over hers, the queen smiling at me from the top, teasingly. I sighed and shook my head, leaning back heavily in my chair.

"This was fun," Rhea said, her guards clearing the table of both of our chips.

"You could have gotten more from me," I said quietly, more confused about her ludicrous request than angry about the loss.

"Believe me," she said, "I got more than you can imagine."

Her smile sent chills down my spine.

***

I woke up the next morning to the sound of banging on my door. Eyes still glazed over, I looked at the time on my cellphone and cursed as I slipped out of bed. The banging continued until I opened the door and was greeted by my doorman.

"What is it?" I was ready to smack him across the face.

"So sorry to wake you up, but is Mr. Mustafa home?"

I scowled at him, immediately hating whatever game he was playing. "I'm Mustafa," I said with clenched teeth. "What do you want, Samir."

"No, I meant the other Mr. Mustafa," Samir said calmly.

"Are you drunk?"

"God forbid," Samir said, shaking his head in anger, clearly insulted. "Please tell Mr. Mustafa that his car is double parked and the lady downstairs can't get out."

"I'm Mustafa!" I shouted at him, not in the mood for playing his game any longer. "I'll be down in a second." I slammed the door in his face and went back to my room to change.

**

The rest of the day was a disaster.

I avoided my doorman, thinking of the best way to apologize for my outburst without encouraging too much discussion about the incident, and started my Friday errands. I passed by the kiosk at the end of my street and was annoyed at how the owner rudely pretended not to know me as he chatted away on his phone, handing me my pack of cigarettes without a second glance. I received the same treatment from the baker and the market attendant I usually got my groceries from, both of whom I was inclined to never to do business with again. When my neighbor ignored my attempts at polite small talk in the elevator, forcing us both to stand in awkward silence as we waited for our respective floors, I came to the conclusion that the whole world had gone crazy.

I called my parents, both of whom didn't answer, and my sister hung up on me as soon as she heard my voice. I decided to pass by them later, trying to remember what I had done wrong. It must have been something minor they had probably blown completely out of proportion. I tried to log into my work email, remembering that I had work left over from Thursday, but couldn't. I tried my personal email, and when that failed, shut my laptop in anger and called Tamer.

"Hello?" He sounded like he had just woken up.

"Did you sleep in? Man, I'm jealous."

35

"Who's this?"

"Check your caller ID, idiot. Listen, I can't log into my work email. Can you see what's wrong with that?"

A long silence ensued.

"Tamer, you there?"

"Who is this?"

I sighed heavily. "Mustafa," I replied. "Can you wake up from whatever stupor you're in? I really need the email to work, man."

"Mustafa who?"

"What do you mean, Mustafa who?" I asked, my voice rising. "The only friend you've ever had. The guy who's going to kick your ass if you don't wake up!"

"Screw you," the reply came, and he hung up. I stood dumbfounded, staring at my phone, unclear as to what had just happened. I dialed again.

"Who is this?" came the sharp reply from the other end.

"Dude, what are you doing?"

"Listen, jackass," Tamer shouted into the phone, clearly awake and at full attention. "I don't know who the hell you think you are, but call me again and it'll be the last time you'll call anyone. I have your number, and I can find you. You really don't want me to do that. Now beat it!"

"What are you—" I started, but he had already hung up.

To say I was confused would be an understatement. I was about to dial again when I thought against it and threw my phone to the side. Tamer was going to realize his mistake soon enough and call to apologize. I just needed to give him to time to fully wake up.

I started to empty out my groceries, thinking about the other day. Although sleep had helped, I still felt confused about the whole ordeal. The game had been fun, that was for sure, but Rhea still confused me. I had hoped a fresh mind would provide a better vantage point, help me see things from a different angle and maybe discern what it was that bothered me, but nothing came. There had to be someone who knew something about this.

I suddenly remembered that I still had Glasses' card. Immediately abandoning the groceries, I raced to the coffee table next to the door and opened my wallet, rummaging through the cards, looking for the slip of paper Tamer had given me. Something caught my eye, and when I looked back through the mix of credit cards and personal ID's, my blood froze.

There was no name.

I quickly emptied out the contents of my wallet onto the table, arranging the cards to one side, trying hard to disbelieve what I was seeing. My personal ID had nothing on it, a blank piece of plastic with just the yellowish background and the face of the sphinx staring up at me. My credit cards shone in their multitude of colors, devoid of any identification as to who owned them. Even my driver's license was blank. It was as if, overnight, my name had been erased completely.

My name.

I froze as the realization hit me, hard and fast, taking me by surprise and knocking the wind out of me. I suddenly felt my entire body shiver, and I slowly sat down on the ground, carefully balancing my descent as something inside me squeezed into a tight knot. I gasped for breath, and realizing that I was having trouble, tried hard to stop the panic attack from coming.

She had taken my name.

***

"We're closed!"

I heard Glasses shout from the back of his store, buried beneath shadows and junk tossed all over. The small room was as uninviting as his voice, the ironic sound of the chimes announcing my visit as I stepped through the door. I looked for him in the heaps of boxed up madness laid out in uneven aisles, and only when he realized that he had gotten no answer and came out to inspect, did I finally see him, shirt sleeves rolled up, frown on his face.

"I said we're closed!"

"I need to talk to you," I said.

He squinted at me, raising his dark glasses to take a better look, then sighed with recognition. "What the hell are *you*

37

doing here?" he asked, bending down to rummage through a few boxes to one side.

"So you know who I am?" I asked.

"It's been one day, boy," he mumbled. "Why wouldn't I know who–" he stopped what he was doing and slowly turned to look at me. "You stupid, stupid boy." His voice was barely a whisper.

"I need your help."

"You bet your name, didn't you?" he demanded, suddenly more interested in me than before, a snarl on his face. "Are you mad? Do you have any idea what you have done?"

"No, I don't," I said, "that's why I'm here."

"You need to leave, right now," he said, grabbing my arm and pushing me towards the door. "You can't be here. If she finds out you're talking to another No Name, she'll be furious!"

"Another what?"

"Out!"

I pulled my arm away and pushed at him, breaking his control over the situation, balling my fists.

"Listen, you dragged us into this, you brought us to that game, and I swear by everything I hold dear, if you don't help me right now I'll make sure I take out every ounce of rage and confusion I've had since this morning on you and your store."

I was getting ready to swing, angry at how dismissive he was being, angrier still at my need for him. He sized me up, then sighed and started wiping his glasses on the ends of his shirt. He looked at the lenses in the little bit of light coming into the small store, and, satisfied, put the rims back on.

"I guess this was bound to happen one day."

***

Glasses led me into the Hanging Church, quiet during the entire subway ride, keeping his eyes to the ground. It was the last train out, his explanation being that once Rhea was done with us, we wouldn't be going home anyway. I had spent four hours drinking tea to the sounds of his bubbling hookah as he shared what he knew, information I had desperately sought and finally regretted knowing.

The Complex of Religions was deserted, its security inexplicably oblivious to our presence as we walked past them. I had been to the Hanging Church several times before, knowing of his historical build over an old Roman fortress. I had marveled at the depths of the passage it had been built over, gazing down with countless other tourists through protected glass floors.

I had never wondered what might be down there.

I followed Glasses into the church, the guard at its door looking at us only momentarily before quickly turning away. I suspected he knew why we were here. I took in the church's nightly magnificence before refocusing at the task at hand.

We walked into the church's nave, quickly strolling past the rows of pews and the pulpit, then turned right through a narrow door into a smaller room. There were more pews, their monotony broken only by a single figure sitting with his back towards us. Glasses stopped, patiently waiting for the man to turn around and face us. Scars greatly disfigured his face. His eyes stared menacingly at us, a peculiar mix with the unusual calm that surrounded him.

"We need to see her," Glasses finally broke the silence.

"That is not permitted," the gruff voice replied.

"Let her be the judge of that," Glasses said impatiently. "Just let her know we're here."

The man cocked his head to a side. The silence that followed was more disturbing than him, and when he finally turned back, I could see he was more agitated than when we had first come in. He walked down the pews to a wall and pressed his hands against it, the stones moving out of place to reveal a staircase.

"This is a violation," he threw in as we walked past him and down the stairs.

"No worries, big guy," Glasses called back over his shoulder.

I followed him down, my hands finding balance on the cold stone walls around me. I felt my foot lose its holding a few times, and was quickly given a disapproving look each time. I knew Glasses was taking a big risk bringing me here, and I believed that even though he knew this was probably the end of the line, he was definitely not thrilled by it.

The stairs ended in a small corridor that opened into the old gate passage, a magnificent space, the only light coming down through the glass floor pieces of the church above. I looked around in awe, feeling very small in a place so old, and only refocused when Glasses nudged me in the side.

At one end of the passage sat Rhea, half-hidden in the shadows, at a table similar to the one we had played on the night before. I could see her smile in the darkness, barely visible, welcoming, yet cold. She was shuffling a deck of cards.

"This is quite surprising, Phillip," she said, her voice echoing off the ancient stone walls. "I would have thought that you, above all, would know the rules."

"The boy wants a rematch," Glasses countered, visibly sweating. Gone was the confidence he had worn throughout the way here.

"The boy has nothing I want."

"I have my name," I said, cutting in before Glasses could say anything else. "I want a rematch."

Rhea leaned over the table, the dim light now fully on her face, and I could see her eyes mocking me. "I believe you know well that I already have that."

"You have my official name," I said. "I was named Ibrahim at birth. My father changed it to Mustafa in honor of his father. I think that might be something you'd like to add to your collection."

I cringed when her smile widened. "I knew you were interesting."

***

I looked at the royal flush in my hand and felt nostalgic.

I had a sickening feeling that history was repeating itself. Looking up at Rhea's smiling face, I remembered Glasses' warning not to trust her. She cheated, he had said, but had assured me that she couldn't do that here. That's why the game had to be here. Still, reading her was impossible, the smile on

Tell Me Your Name

her face unchanging as if painted there, her expression a mask I could not see past.

I looked down at my hand again and worried that coming here might have been a mistake. I couldn't take solace in the fact that I was luckier than most, because when push came to shove, luck was never on my side. I thought hard and long before finally giving in to temptation and asking to change three cards.

Rhea dealt the cards quickly, and then leaned over to say, "Are you sure about this?"

I didn't answer, looking at the three new cards lying face down on the table. I looked at Glasses and found no support in the sweaty face watching us.

"Your hand?" I asked, pushing through with the plan.

"You don't want to see your cards?"

"It doesn't matter," I said. "The stakes aren't changing. It can go either way."

Rhea smiled and laid her cards down, her full house mocking me as she leaned back and smiled. I cursed the fact that I had had a higher hand and had let it go. I reached over with a sinking heart to look at my new cards. Picking them up one by one, I felt relief rush through me.

I threw down the queen, and watched Rhea's smile disappear as she saw the trump card.

"The boy's lucky after all," Glasses said, letting out a long breath he had been holding in. I could see the tension leave his body as well, a glimpse of his confidence returning.

"Indeed, he is," Rhea said. "Still, a deal's a deal. Your name will be returned to you."

"No," I said.

Rhea stared me straight in the eye. "What do you mean, no?" she almost hissed.

"I never said I wanted my name back."

"Then what do you want?"

"I want yours."

Rhea's smile returned. "It is quite an exotic name. I can see why you want it."

"I don't want Rhea," I shook my head. "I want your real name."

41

The smile faded again and she quickly looked at Glasses, her eyes throwing daggers at him.

"You see, I hear that you're just like me, with an unofficial name of your own," I smirked. Rhea looked back at me, her mouth drawn back in a snarl. "I want your name."

"Don't push it, boy," Rhea hissed. "You know nothing of what you're getting yourself into."

"Tell me your name," I said, my tone harsher, my confidence stronger.

From somewhere below me, a rumbling came.

"Change your request," she ordered.

"Tell me your name!"

I suddenly felt the earth around me shake, the rumbling growing louder as she got up from her seat. "Change your request!"

I held onto the table as the shaking threatened to throw me off my seat. Glasses got up and backed away from the table, looking around for a way out, trying to keep his balance.

"Tell me your name!"

She lunged at me. I felt a sudden fear in the pit of my stomach as I saw her face crack, her expression changing to that of a rabid dog, her claw-like fingers aimed at my face. Suddenly, she was jerked back, and she screeched as she tried to break free from whatever invisible force was keeping her from me.

"You maggot!" she screamed at me. "You fool. You are nothing. You are dust. You are but a speck of dirt in comparison to the forces you mess with. I will have your heart!"

"Tell me your name!"

The earth shook harder, and I jumped to a side as a rock crashed down beside me. I could feel the walls of the old fortress buckling, the strain of the shaking threatening to collapse the entire structure.

"I am above you. How dare you ask for my name?"

"Tell me your name!"

Her scream was deafening, echoing off the walls in a magnifying screech that forced me to cover my ears. More cracks appeared on her face, and I could see something horrible behind them, something I knew was better left hidden.

"I am She Who Has No Name," she howled. "I am The Collector, The Immortal, She Who Is Everyone!"

"Your name!"

"I am Jack, Jason, Lee, Agatha, Louis," she chanted. "I am Amun, Maximus, Kimera, and Sultan!"

"Your name!"

"I am One, I am All!"

"Your name!"

The cracks appeared across her neck, running across her body, her skin breaking and falling like a broken china doll. Her body shook with the earth under my feet, and somewhere inside me, I knew I was going to lose my control over the situation. I could see Rhea's body twist in angles I never knew were possible, writhing with pain. I ran to her, grabbed her, and pushed her against a wall.

"Tell me your name!"

"Aedelpryd!" she hissed in my face, her breath rotten. "My name is Aedelpryd!"

Rhea exploded to pieces in my hands.

***

I looked at the man sitting across from me and smiled.

The night had gone well, and my chips were lined high to one side. The rest of the guests had left, whimpering at their loss, some cursing my luck while others cursing me. I understood how they felt. Only one remained, and he was good. Reading him was hard.

I looked at my hand and couldn't help but smile.

"Let's make this a little more interesting," I said, and threw in all my chips.

"I don't have that much," the man said. "I only have cash."

"I don't want your money," I said, my smile widening.

"I'm afraid I really have nothing else."

I folded my cards and leaned in towards him. "How about you just throw in your name?"

Tell Me Your Name

* * *

His Neighbor's Garden
By Ron Ripley

Larry hated his next-door neighbor.

He had ever since he and his wife had moved in ten years before. And, since Janet had left him at Christmas, the hatred had only increased. By leaps and bounds.

Larry stood in his kitchen, coffee mug in hand, as he looked out of the window behind the sink. From his position, he could see over his weather-stained lawn furniture and down into Joan's garden. It was the proverbial riot of color.

Hundreds of brilliant and various-shaded flowers, spilled out of the narrow beds. Long stems and broad leaves fluttered in the gentle summer breeze. Even through the glass of his window, Larry imagined he could smell the sickeningly sweet aroma of the blossoms. He took a drink, found the coffee had grown cold and spit it into the sink. Angrily, he emptied the mug, rinsed it out and shoved it into the drying rack.

He looked out into Joan's garden again and saw the woman's mongrel dog. The creature, a mix between a pug and a beagle, wandered along the path made of Belgian paving stones. Larry watched furiously as the dog neared the invisible boundary between his yard and Joan's.

The dog hesitated, then made its way into Larry's yard, trotted over to his favorite Adirondack chair and proceeded to urinate on it.

Pure, unhindered rage filled Larry, and he turned away from the sink. His bare feet slapped against the cold tile of the floor, and when he reached the back door, he ripped it open. The knob slipped out of his hand, banging loudly off the wall. Larry pushed the screen door open, stomped down the steps and into his yard.

The dog saw him, its tail dropping down between its legs. Larry watched as it scurried back into Joan's yard, vanishing beneath a bright yellow forsythia bush.

"Oh no, you don't," Larry hissed, chasing after it. He followed the path, the paving stones painfully cold beneath his feet. Larry muttered to himself, got down on his hands and

45

knees and peered under the bush. The dog slipped away, vanishing through the branches on the far side.

With a grunt, Larry pushed himself up, his stomach getting in the way momentarily, and the realization of how fat he was made him even angrier.

His blood pounded in his head as he went around the bush and saw the dog. Its tail had curled up, and the dog looked at him as if taunting him, daring him to go further into Joan's well-manicured and large yard.

"Try and hide, you little mutt!" Larry spat. He hurried after the dog, traveling deeper into the garden. The dog wove through trees and large bushes, Larry barely able to keep up. Within a few minutes, he was breathing hard, looking around as he came to a stop.

Go home, a small voice told him.

No, Larry thought. *I'm going to teach it a lesson. It won't be coming back into my yard for a while.*

While he stood, trying to decide what to do, Larry heard someone singing. He couldn't make out the words, but the tone, the musicality of the voice pulled at him. Without knowing why, Larry took a step forward. He tilted his head and listened.

Then the song stopped and the air grew heavier, the humidity increasing.

Why did they stop singing? Larry thought numbly. He staggered forward, confused. Above him, the tree branches were woven together, leaves blocking the morning sun, putting the entire garden into a deep shade.

A pair of lilac bushes appeared in front of him, the dog squirming between them.

Larry shook his head and barreled in after it, the branches scratching him and drawing blood. Finally, he stumbled into an open area and came to a sharp stop. He swayed unsteadily on his feet, looking around him.

A small expanse, encircled by lilacs, held a little pool with a stone bench beside it. The air was cold, and the dog was gone. Carefully, Larry stepped forward. The glade muffled the sound of his footsteps, and hid his hoarse breathing from his ears.

His anger had eased, and as he looked around, he realized he had gone farther into Joan's yard than he had intended.

Wait, Larry thought, looking around. *Her yard isn't this big. What the hell is going on?*

A splash sounded in the water, and Larry focused on it. Ripples spread out across the surface, and when Larry neared it, he could see shapes. Giant coy fish swam lazily, and one great white and orange one drifted up and snapped at a bug in the water. In the depths of the pool, the fish he thought were small became considerably larger, as if the water was far deeper than it looked.

How deep does it go? Larry wondered. He couldn't see the bottom of the pool. *Is it an illusion? Seriously, how the hell is it so deep?*

At the edge of his vision, Larry saw a shape appear in the water. The fish moved easily along the wall, far below the level of the others. The coy scattered the closer it came, and soon Larry was able to discern curly hair. It floated around the creature's head, a strong tail snapping left and right. The coy vanished, swimming deeper, avoiding the new arrival.

The new fish looked up, and Larry couldn't tear his eyes away.

What looked like a mermaid was swimming towards him.

Her hair was black, her skin pale. Her eyes were set wide, no eyebrows. The nose was small and flat. Each lip was thin and light pink. She was topless, and she moved towards him without any sense of decency. Her arms were well muscled, the fingers long, thin and webbed.

She swam up to the top of the pool, without breaking the surface. Light blue eyes, full of lust and seduction, looked at him.

Larry heard a rustle behind him and twisted around.

Joan walked into the small glade, her dog beside her.

Larry's anger spiked. "You need to control your damned dog, Joan!"

Joan looked at him. "You should mind own business, Larry. Cerebus told me you were running around, chasing him."

"Sure he did," Larry said. He looked at the woman in front of him. She wore a light blue housecoat which hung on her small frame. Her white hair was pulled back in a ponytail, the bones of her face highlighted by the thinness of her flesh and skin. She smoothed out her housecoat with nimble hands free of arthritis.

"You need to leave now," Joan said. Her voice was as cold as the air in the glade.

Larry shook his head. "No. I don't think so. Not until I know what you have in there."

"Where?" Joan asked.

He jerked his thumb towards the pond. "What the hell is that? And where did you get it?"

"You've seen her?" Joan said softly.

"How could I miss it?" he asked, scoffing.

"Her name is Nya," Joan said coldly. "She is a she and most certainly not an *it*."

"Whatever," Larry said dismissively. "Why don't you tell me where you caught it?"

Anger flashed across Joan's face. "I didn't catch *her*, I saved her, years ago."

"Where?" Larry asked. *I wonder how much someone would pay for a damned mermaid.*

"In a lake in Maine," Joan said. She sat down on the ground, patted the dog on its head and smiled when it climbed into her lap.

Disgusting, Larry thought, shuddering with revulsion. "Are there more of them?"

"Undoubtedly," Joan said.

"How come they haven't been caught before?" he demanded.

"They're smart," Joan said. "And I told you, I didn't catch her. I helped her. She chose to stay with me."

He shook his head. "Sure she did. How did you 'help' her?"

"She was only a child," Joan said, smiling at the pool. "Nothing more. I found her lost along the shore. She was sick, and I nursed her back to health. Nya has been with me ever since."

"Not for long," Larry said, chuckling. "Do you have any idea how much money I'm going to make off of this little mermaid of yours?"

"She's no mermaid," Joan said coldly. "She's a siren. A dangerous creature, meant to end the likes of you."

"Sure," Larry said, chuckling. He glanced at the pool, saw the young girl as she hovered beneath the water's surface and smiled at her. She returned it, and there was a promise of pleasure, if only he'd bring her up.

I'll bring you up, Larry thought. *Maybe keep you for myself for a while.*

"You need to leave," Joan said. "Go. It is in her nature to drown men, and I would have you leave this place alive rather than dead."

"Sure," Larry said, laughing. "Sure. Listen, I'm going to bring this little lady up and out of the water. Maybe show her what she's been missing, and then put her on the daytime talk show circuit."

Joan looked hard at Larry, put the dog down, and got to her feet. She took slow, small steps towards him. Her eyes, which matched the blue of her housecoat, never left his face. Larry swallowed uncomfortably, suddenly nervous.

"Stay where you are," he said, taking half a step back. "You need to stay away from me."

"Afraid of an old woman?" she asked softly. "I'm ninety-two years old. How can you be afraid of me?"

Joan moved closer with every word until she was no more than a foot away from him. She looked up into his face and gave him a cold smile. Her teeth were small, yellowed with age, and disturbing to see up close.

"And, Larry," Joan whispered, "you're trespassing."

She pointed at him with a ridiculously small index finger and poked him in the chest.

Cold, wet hands grabbed his ankles, and suddenly Joan pushed against him with both hands planted firmly on his chest. The dog barked loudly, a sharp, yipping sound.

Larry tried to stand, but the hands on his ankles pulled, and Joan grabbed two handfuls of his shirt and threw herself against him.

He tumbled backward, and Joan didn't let go. Together they spilled into the pool, the chilly water making Larry gasp. The weight of the old woman on his chest pushed him down as Nya, her hands unrelenting, pulled him deeper into the pool.

Larry thrashed against both of them, the mermaid and the woman.

His lungs screamed for oxygen as he kicked down viciously, finally freeing his legs of Nya's tenacious grasp. The creature grinned at him, latched onto him again, and opened her mouth. Sharp teeth flashed at him in the curious light of the pool, and she pulled him closer. Larry twisted around, lashed out with a foot and smashed the siren on the side of her head. Nya went limp and slowly drifted towards the unseen bottom of the pool.

With the mermaid gone, Larry focused on the old woman, reaching down and grabbing her fingers. He felt them break as he bent them back and Larry shoved her under him as he scrambled to the surface.

Joan tried to follow him up, grasping at him, but Larry continued to kick at her. Her eyes bulged from their sockets and he could see her struggle to hold her breath. He aimed a final blow at her face, and managed to kick her solidly in the jaw. Joan's mouth opened involuntarily, and she doubled over as she took in a great lungful of water. Bubbles raced out of her mouth and she twisted around.

Larry watched for a moment as she drifted down, her body still and limp in the water.

As he launched himself up, freeing himself of the water, Larry took in shuddering gasps of breath.

His arms ached as he grabbed hold of the pool's edge and dragged himself out. Shivers raced through him, his clothes wet and heavy on his flesh. Panting, he turned around and looked at the water feature. Cautiously, he crept towards it, lifted himself up and peered over the edge.

In the clear water, there was no sign of either Joan or the mermaid.

Oh thank God, Larry thought. He pushed himself away from the pool, far enough so he could catch his breath without the fear of being dragged back in.

A whimper reached his ear, and Larry looked towards the sound. The old woman's mongrel dog lay on its side, convulsing. Foam clung to its muzzle, and the eyes had rolled back to reveal the whites.

Larry sneered at the dog and got to his feet, swaying slightly.

There was the sound of something ripping, and Larry turned his attention back to the dog.

The mongrel's fur had torn along the length of the spine. A black pelt, wet and gleaming, greeted Larry's eyes. The dog let out a horrific howl, and its coat was shredded as the flesh beneath it expanded. Larry's sneer changed to a mask of terror as the dog *grew*.

It was no longer a small mixed breed, but a large dog, easily the size of a Great Dane.

And when it lifted its neck, there were three heads instead of one.

Joan's mutt got to its feet, the trio of noses quivering, lips pulling back to reveal white, jagged teeth. Three pairs of bright yellow eyes locked onto Larry, and three deep, powerful howls pierced the air.

Larry spun on his heel and ran. When he reached the edge of the small glade, he faintly heard a splash, and a moment later, Nya's voice filled the air.

The song was arresting, harsh and seductive all in one breath. Larry reacted to it instantly, staggering to a stop just before the safety of the bushes. He straightened up and listened to Nya's song.

Then the beast was on him.

The dog slammed into the small of his back, knocking him to the ground. The air rushed out of Larry's lungs as one set of teeth dug into the flesh around his spine. A heartbeat later, he was lifted off the ground, the dog shaking him as it would a rat.

Bones cracked, and muscles tore. With a vicious jerk, the dog severed something in Larry's spine, and he couldn't see anymore. Larry felt himself being dropped to the ground and then being rolled over onto his back.

Larry screamed as teeth latched onto his shoulder and he was dragged a short distance. The dog let go, and Larry sobbed, trying to move but unable to do so.

I'm dying! he thought frantically. *Oh, Jesus Christ, I'm dying!*

How long? How long is it going to take?

Then cold, wet hands wrapped around his neck and dragged him into the pool. As Larry struggled to breathe a small voice in his head whispered, *Not long at all, Larry. Not long at all.*

And the voice was right.

* * *

The Sin Eater
By David Longhorn

He lived in a hut on a bleak hillside, and was despised.

Nobody knew his name, or how old he was, or where he even came from. If he'd ever had family in the neighborhood, they were either long gone or kept quiet about their link to the outcast. When people met him on the roads or in the fields they turned aside, some saying a prayer, others mouthing a charm passed down from an older tradition. Children sometimes taunted him, the braver ones even threw stones, but only till an adult came and drove them away. Everyone knew it was bad luck to lay eyes on the nameless man, to spend even the briefest time within sight of him.

The Sin-Eater was one of many boogeymen invoked by weary parents to keep fractious children quiet. He just happened to be real.

He had only one function, and when he was needed, the people of the district did not need to seek him out. Some uncanny instinct told the Sin-Eater when he could enter a home where a wake was being held. It was his role to eat a simple meal from a wooden bowl placed on the chest of the corpse, and to take upon himself all the sins of any dead man, woman, or child. It was believed this would speed the passage of the deceased through purgatory to paradise. Once he had finished his meal, the Sin-Eater would return to his hovel, and the ritual would be complete.

The bowl, especially crafted for the occasion, was always burned afterwards.

"He is the last of his kind," mused the parish priest, with a sad shake of the head. He often regretted the passing of the old ways, although they clashed with his own beliefs. More than that, though, he wished he could in some way improve the lot of the outcast on the hill, the meanest of his flock. As things stood, he did what little he could.

It was customary for the parish priest to leave food and drink for the Sin-Eater by the churchyard gate on the first day of the month. The Reverend Monckton stood, now, awaiting the nameless man, feeling it is his duty to make sure that the provisions were not taken by just any passing vagrant. A thin rain fell, the last remnant of storms over the Welsh hills to the west.

"I really think you are indulging these people's superstitions," grumbled the squire, who had come to chat with his old friend and disliked all concessions to the old ways.

Sir John Prescott was a forward-thinking man, an advocate of science, education, and progress. He had been instrumental in bringing the railway and the telegraph to his remote corner of Herefordshire. Not surprisingly, Sir John felt sin-eating, like witchcraft and fortune-telling, was a worthless relic of the Dark Ages. This was the Year of Our Lord 1889, a time of enlightenment. With the British Empire engaged in spreading civilization to the four corners of the globe, no decent Victorian gentleman could overlook the backwardness of the English peasantry.

Thanks to his forward-looking attitude, Sir John's tenants had been provided with clean water and their offspring with proper schooling. The squire had even tried to vaccinate them, desisting only when the priest warned him he might face an open revolt over the issue. There had already been ominous mutterings when a steam-thresher was introduced at harvest time. Reluctantly, Sir John had postponed the vaccination program.

"You are a little hard on these people, my friend," said the priest, taking up the well-worn topic. "They cling to familiar customs in a fast-changing, uncertain world. We all need reassurance, and the less power we have over our fates the more we need. And remember, it is essentially tradition that keeps us in our privileged roles in our little community. Just as it keeps that poor soul in his."

Monckton nodded towards the hills, and Sir John looked out into the drizzle. Sure enough, the Sin-Eater was coming. The man moved like a living scarecrow, a painfully thin figure clad in rags, limping along the muddy country lane that led past the church. He kept his head down, so that the brim of a slouch-hat shaded his face, most of which was concealed by a wild growth of hair and beard anyway.

"Disgraceful!" snorted Sir John. "Such a poor, deranged simpleton should be in a hospital or asylum, not living wild in the hills!"

The landowner turned away in disgust and went inside the church. The priest stayed in the porch, sheltered from the rain, watching the nameless man eat and drink just outside consecrated ground. Monckton knew the Sin-Eater, his status lower than a leper, could never trespass on a holy place. Indeed, the pariah could enter no place where decent folk dwelt, except at the one special time when he performed his role in rural society.

The outcast finished his simple meal then stood upright, facing the church porch where the priest stood looking on. The ragged slouch-hat shadowed the man's face, but Monckton caught the slight glimmer of two deep-set eyes.

Does he believe it? Monckton wondered. *Does he really feel the sins of the dead entering his body, his soul, when he eats that meager meal? Heretical to even think it, of course, but still, his faith must be at least as strong as mine. Ah, but the poor devil!*

The priest wanted to go to the gate and talk to the Sin-Eater, ask him about his life, his torments, perhaps offer some spiritual solace. But he knew better. His parishioners would know and attendance at his services would drop. Monckton would lose face, perhaps even be ostracized by some of the older folk. It had happened before to unwise clergy.

The nameless man who ate the sins of others was a thing of evil, by definition. How could he be otherwise, with such a burden of wrongdoing all locked up inside? Talking to him would be polluting oneself with the sins he bore. So instead, the priest raised a tentative hand in greeting. At first, the man outside the churchyard gave no sign that he had seen the gesture. Then the Sin-Eater nodded, turned, and walked back the way he had come. Soon, he was out of sight, and the priest went into the church to join his friend.

"Scuttled back to his burrow, eh?" asked Sir John, rising stiffly from a bench. "Gone to earth like an animal! Pah!"

"No matter how wretched he may be, he is still a man, a child of God, with an immortal soul just like you and I," chided the priest, gently.

For a moment, the squire looked as if he would take offense at being likened to a ragged halfwit at the bottom of the social ladder. But Sir John could never be angry with his friend for long. He grinned and punched the priest lightly on the shoulder.

"Of course, you're right, Philip," he mumbled in embarrassment. "I sometimes forget my Christian duty. You do your best for that poor fellow, just as I try to help the villagers. It's not easy to improve the lot of people who seem so mired in medieval superstition, though."

"Let's change the subject, John," said the priest, leading his friend through to the vestry where they could sit without fear of interruption. Monckton produced a bottle of whiskey and poured out a couple of glasses, to 'keep the chill out', as he always put it. A few moments' silence followed as they contemplated the single malt.

"Now that is what the Scots call 'a good swalley'," observed Sir John.

"Indeed," said the priest, refilling both glasses, "sometimes a nice, hot cup of tea is not enough to satisfy the inner man."

Sir John, whose mood had brightened after taking the liquor, frowned.

"No, but strong drink does a lot of harm, Philip, let us not overlook that."

Monckton sighed. Another difficult topic had reared its head.

"I take it that Victor is not faring well in his medical career?" he asked.

The squire's nephew, adopted after the boy's parents perished in a shipwreck on their way back from India, had long been a source of anxiety to Sir John. As an old bachelor set in his ways he had struggled to raise his younger brother's son with the right balance of kindness and discipline. Sir John had tried to make Victor honest and hard-working, while Monckton had tried to make him a good Christian. Both had failed. Before Victor had gone to London, there had been several ugly incidents involving servant girls that had cost Sir John a fair sum to smooth over.

The priest recalled Victor's eyes. They were cunning, malign, and somehow inhuman, like the eyes of a reptile that had been raised to human intelligence. He shuddered.

"It's kind of you to put it so tactfully, Philip," said the squire, gazing into his whiskey glass. "But the boy seems to have sunk further into depravity. I know he neglects his studies. I had a letter from the teaching hospital, telling me he will be thrown off the course for non-attendance of lectures. Instead he writes to me for money and spends it in the East End on Lord knows what. Judging by his handwriting, he's a drunkard. Or worse."

"We're both men of the world," said Monckton, trying to be tactful. "We know the young must let off steam in some way or another. We did, after all, in our different ways. And there are far worse things to do in London than get drunk."

Even as he spoke, the priest realized that he had blundered. The squire's brow furrowed. *No doubt he's thinking of London's other snares for unwary young men. I should change the subject.*

"Perhaps Victor is simply not cut out to be a surgeon?"

Sir John laughed.

"An unfortunate turn of phrase, there, but I fear you're right. Last week, I wrote and told him that he must return here and face me, tell me what he does want to do. He should be arriving tomorrow, by the midday train. Perhaps you could do me the favor of calling round in the afternoon, provide me with a little moral support?"

The priest nodded, forced a smile. He had no wish to be reacquainted with Victor, but he would do his best for his friend.

"Try not to lose your temper with the lad, John. It's not easy for a boy to become a man these days. The young are under terrible pressures, of a sort we were spared in more sedate times."

Squire and priest talked a little longer, then parted amicably. After locking up, Reverend Monckton paused at the

57

gate of the churchyard to check on the remains of the Sin-Eater's meal. A few crusts of bread and pieces of fruit-peel lay in an earthenware bowl. An old, chipped jug that had been filled with rough cider was empty.

After a moment's thought, the priest smashed the bowl and the jug against the gatepost. Just in case anyone was watching.

***

The next afternoon, the priest walked to the manor house from his parsonage, hoping to find uncle and nephew reconciled, or at least on speaking terms. His route took him through the village, and as usual he greeted members of his flock as they went about their business. At first, he didn't notice anything unusual, but then Monckton realized that there was a general movement along the main street, in the same direction that he was taking. What's more, people were wearing their Sunday best on a Saturday, the women in fine bonnets and skirts, the men in black suits. One laborer, a talkative old chap, noticed the priest's puzzled expression and fell in beside him.

"You haven't heard the news then, have you, Reverend?"

"About what, Jethro?" asked Monckton.

"Squire's nephew has died!" replied Jethro with relish, pleased to be the bearer of bad tidings.

"Aye!" chimed in a woman, falling into step with them. "Lad were found dead by the ticket inspector when the train arrived at Hereford! Laid out on the floor of the carriage, he were! Police brought the body to the hall just afore midday!"

My poor friend, thought Monckton. *His only blood relation, his sole heir, dead!*

"Excuse me, I must hurry!" he said, quickening his pace.

The priest arrived at the manor ahead of most of the villagers, but there was still a line of men and women standing outside the Grange, waiting to pay their respects as was the custom. To his credit, Sir John was standing on the steps of the fine portico, speaking to each of his tenants in turn. Monckton felt a wave of sympathy for his old friend, knowing how much the squire must have wanted to lock himself away from the world at this moment.

The gathered locals stepped aside to make way for the priest, murmuring polite greetings, doffing caps. They were watching, of course, and Monckton was careful not to betray any feeling before the villagers. He and Sir John exchanged nods, shook hands, then the squire said,

"Please, go inside. He is in–"

Sir John stopped, began again with a catch in his voice.

"His body is laid out in the drawing room."

Monckton went inside, leaving his friend to receive more condolences from his tenants. A servant ushered him silently into the library, where the curtains had been drawn against the afternoon sunshine. Oil lamps and candles cast a sickly light over the body of the young man. The priest leaned over to look at the pale, clean-shaven face.

Even in death there is no repose, he thought. *He always seemed such an unquiet soul, unable to relax. One can only hope that he has now found solace in the bosom of Our Savior.*

Monckton said a brief prayer, made the sign of the cross over the corpse, then walked out into the hallway of the manor. As he did so, he heard a commotion outside, voices raised in surprised, alarm, perhaps even fear. He hurried to the doorway and looked out.

The number of people waiting to pay their respects to their squire had grown, with nearly a hundred men and women gathered outside the Grange. The crowd was parting, now, just as it had done to let the priest through minutes before. But this time it was not out of respect that the villagers moved. No, they stepped aside hastily, some colliding or stumbling, every man and woman afraid to come too close to the Sin-Eater.

The outcast walked slowly up the drive towards the great house. He moved painfully, limping, and Monckton saw that the man had no shoes, merely rags wrapped round his feet. His clothes were filthy and torn. The broad brim of his hat again shadowed his face.

Sir John did not stand aside for the Sin-Eater.

The nameless man limped slowly up the three deep stone steps onto the portico, then stopped in front of the squire. Monckton hurried forward to stand next to his friend, took Sir John's arm. He felt the quivering tension in the squire and, afraid that violence might ensue, he whispered urgently,

"Please, John, let the man in, I beg of you! He can do no harm!"

Sir John looked around, his face bloodless with shock.

"Philip, how can I let that – that thing near the poor lad?"

The priest gripped the squire's arm even more tightly.

"You must, John! They will not forgive you if you do not! Do this for me, John, if you won't do it for yourself!"

A long minute passed as the two men stared unblinking at each other. Monckton heard whispering among the tenants. The Sin-Eater stood still as the scarecrow he resembled. The priest wondered if the man could speak at all. After all, he had had no-one to talk to for decades.

"Very well," said Sir John, and the priest released his grip. The squire turned and strode inside, ordering a servant to prepare a plate of cold beef, then take it to the priest. His way clear, the Sin-Eater limped inside and, without being told, went straight into the library. Monckton followed to find the man standing over the body, looking down with his customary lack of expression.

"The meal will be along shortly," said the priest. There was no indication the Sin-Eater had heard him. What seemed like hours passed as the priest wondered why Sir John's kitchen staff was taking so long to prepare a simple repast. Monckton became aware of the pounding of his own blood in his ears. He also noticed an unpleasant smell, one of sweat and worse. It was the Sin-Eater, a man who had gone unwashed for years, if not decades.

To his relief the cook appeared with a plate heaped with cold meat, handed it to the priest, and then hurried away without looking at the nameless man. She was a local woman. The priest walked up to the table where the body lay and placed the plate carefully on the young man's narrow chest, then stepped back.

The Sin-Eater didn't move.

60

Monckton wondered if there was some invitation he had neglected to make. But none of the accounts he had heard mentioned a form of words needed to begin the meal. *I can hardly say Grace,* he thought.

More time passed, and the priest wondered if he should simply leave. Perhaps his presence as a man of the cloth was blocking the ritual? But leaving the Sin-Eater alone with his friend's nephew felt like a betrayal, somehow. Undecided, he stood looking down at the plate of unappetizing flesh. Again the sound of his own heartbeat filled Monckton's ears.

And then he heard something else. The sound of a woman screaming. Perhaps it was coming from outside, one of the village women having hysterics? Then, just as suddenly as they had started, the screaming stopped.

Monckton looked around the room, seeing nothing, then back at the Sin-Eater. The man had raised his eyes from the corpse and was looking straight at the priest. For the first time, the outcast's face had a clear, recognizable expression. It was utter despair. The deep-set eyes were those of a damned soul, and for one timeless moment, the priest questioned all his most cherished beliefs.

What if it's true? Perhaps he does take sins of the dead onto himself, he thought. *If so, this man must be in Hell here on earth!*

Monckton took a step back, and half-raised a hand as if to ward off an assault. The Sin-Eater smiled, then, his mouth barely visible through a tangle of untamed beard. Then the nameless man stooped over the corpse and began to scoop up the meat with dirt-blackened fingers. The priest looked away, tried to block out the sound of chewing and gulping.

No, it's all nonsense! Absurd to be so affected by this, he told himself. *Of course one must not despise the beliefs of the lower orders, but one must be firm on matters of faith. This is all pure superstition!*

Soon the ancient ritual was over, and the Sin-Eater stood silently for a moment, licking grease off his hands. Then he left, passing the priest without a backward glance. The villagers stood aside again as the pariah walked down the driveway and out of the grounds. He had taken on yet more evil, had become even more despised. There was a collective sigh of relief as the Sin-Eater disappeared along the road that led to his hovel in the hills. Chatter broke out, quiet out of respect for the dead, but obviously tinged with relief. The ritual had been followed. Priest and squire had shown respect for the most important of the old ways.

Monckton raised his hands for attention, put on his best Sunday service voice as he spoke from the top of the steps.

"Good people! Thank you for coming to offer your condolences to Sir John. He is most grateful for your kind thoughts, but hopes you will forgive him if he spends the rest of this sad day in private prayer and contemplation."

The local left, approving the sentiment, and the priest reflected that Sir John might find it easier to innovate in future. *Perhaps he'll even get them vaccinated next year,* he thought. Going indoors he sought out of his friend, and found him in the drawing room sitting before a dead fire, contemplating a heap of luggage.

"His things?" asked Monckton, pointing at the bags.

Sir John nodded.

"Do they know how he died?"

The squire looked up, and his eyes filled with tears.

"The police found a bottle of poison when they searched the railway carriage. It had rolled under the seat. It was easy for him to obtain it from the medical school."

"Suicide? But no, surely he wouldn't–" began Monckton.

Sir John stood up, not looking his friend in the eye.

"Philip, look through his things for me. I can't bear to. My brother's son, I swore to protect him! Perhaps you'll find something that will explain this terrible incident."

The squire's voice broke, then.

"If you can't, I will have to assume that Victor killed himself rather than face me, my anger, my lack of understanding. Please, find another explanation."

For a while, the priest sat alone, contemplating the small heap of worldly possessions. Then he opened the first traveling bag and began to search through it. He found no diary or letters, nothing to fill in the story of the young man's final days. The second bag was no more helpful. All that was left was the medical bag, which of course contained only surgical instruments and vials of drugs.

No, there's something else here.

Monckton reached into a side pocket and found some folded newspaper clippings. He unfolded it on a small table and began to read. It was not difficult to work out the common factor. Even here in the backward west of England there had been widespread fascination with the biggest news story of the last twelve months. The priest scanned the all-too-familiar headlines.

HAS WHITECHAPEL KILLER CLAIMED NEW VICTIM?

'SHOCKING MUTILATION' OF MURDERED WOMAN

POLICE TAUNTED BY 'JACK THE RIPPER'!

Monckton looked up from the clippings. Then he leaned over the medical student's bag again and, moving very carefully, took out one of the instruments he had glanced at a minute earlier. He stood up and took it closer to the window, turned it over in the sunlight.

There were flecks of brown matter on the narrow steel blade.

"Proves nothing," he muttered. "Victor had a morbid imagination, that's all. Young men are often prone to such things."

He put the scalpel back into the bag, locked it. Then he picked up the newspaper cuttings and shoved them into his coat pocket.

"We will never know why he did it," he declared to his reflection in the mirror above the fireplace. Then, more firmly,

"Some things we were not meant to know, John. But we *do* know that God is merciful to us all, whatever our sins. That must be our consolation in times of trouble."

Monckton took a deep breath and prepared to go in search of the squire. Then something stopped him in his tracks. He recalled the moment when the screams had filled the library, before the Sin-Eater took his meal as payment.

Took on his newest burden.

"Proves nothing!" the priest repeated. "Nothing whatsoever!"

He tried not to think of the nameless man taking onto himself the sins of a monster in human form. So many years of taking on the petty wrongdoing of humble peasants, the commonplace lusts and envies and rages of village life. And he tried not to remember his last sight of the Sin-Eater's face, the eyes like those of a reptile, devoid of all human feeling.

"No! The idea is absurd, unscientific, irreligious, and I will not countenance it!"

Again, his reflection looked unconvinced.

* * *

Kimberly
By Sara Clancy

It wasn't an accident.

Everyone just liked to say that it was, telling me repeatedly over the years that I hadn't done anything wrong. That I hadn't meant to hurt him. I think they thought if they said it often enough that I would question the memories of my five-year-old self and believe it too. But I remember. And it wasn't an accident. I had known what would happen when I had grabbed the wheel. I had meant to kill him.

Maybe that was why people were so desperate for me to forget. They didn't want me growing up under a shadow of guilt. But it's my memories that keep me from feeling anything. I remember how rough and dry his hands were when he had pulled me into the car. I remember the exact shade of blue of his eyes, the cut of the knife as he put it to my throat, and the stench that clung to him like a cloud. He had called me 'little love,' had told me I looked 'so sweet.' I remember the hollow feeling I had felt the day I learnt what he had done with all the other children he had taken before me.

He ate them.

There was no polite or gentle way to put it, trust me, a thousand people have tried. I had been lucky, a police officer had been house hunting and had decided to check out the property across from my home. Right place, right time, and after a few excruciating hours in a car hurtling away from the ever growing number of pursuers, I had grabbed the wheel. I survived, he didn't, and no one knew where to go from there.

That was years ago and, while things might never be the same again, life had settled into something that could resemble normalcy. I had pushed that day into some dark back corner of my mind. I had stopped asking why he had chosen me, and my parents had stopped asking why they hadn't been able to prevent it. We moved to a new town and, a few years after that, my parents had a second child, another girl, who shared my large brown eyes and dimples. I took quickly to being a big sister and discovered that I had a lot more patience than I would have thought. She was small and sweet and completely ignorant as to what had happened to me. We decided to keep it that way. There was no reason for her to know, to ever know.

Everything was fine. Not perfect, but calm and peaceful. We were happy. But then, while I had been practicing for my driver's license, someone ran a red light. My little sister, Kimberly, strapped in the baby seat in the back and my father in the passenger seat. We had been lucky, no one had been seriously hurt, no real damage done, but it had been enough to bring the shadow of the past back to my family. After that stupid fender bender and the following dash to the hospital, it had been hard to keep the man from our thoughts. We tried, for Kimberly's sake, and I think my parents still think we had succeeded in carefully containing her innocence. They needed to believe that. I think that's why I never told them that, soon after the accident, Kimberly had taken to climbing into my bed in the middle of the night. She used to curl up into a little ball against my spine, her face pressed against my shoulder blades.

She had done it so often that I had learnt to stop turning to the soft creak of my door opening. I would just yawn, pat the mattress behind me, and say something along the lines of 'come on, then', although looking back I can't remember exactly. The dip of the mattress became a normal sensation and she would often kick me more than once as she settled. Most of the memories of those nights are fuzzy with a sleepy haze, and I can't remember details. But I do remember one night. I had been comfortable and warm, and sleep had been a promise only a few seconds away from actuality when Kimberly's little voice broke the silence.

"Do you remember the time we were in a car accident?"

I vaguely remember smiling. She had often asked things like that. "Of course I do, dummy. It was only a few days ago."

"No, not that time," Kimberly had whispered. "That other time."

At this, my eyes had snapped open and I had stared at the wall straight ahead. I tried to brush it off by muttering something along the lines of, "What other time?"

"That other time," she had insisted with a childish whine. "That time when I was hurt."

Kimberly

"We weren't hurt, Kimberly."

I can still feel the way she pressed into my shoulder as she mumbled, "You weren't, but I was."

At that, I had spun around to face her. The blankets had twisted up around my legs and the whole bed had shook, but Kimberly had barely stirred. She had given me a sleepy smile, closed her eyes, and quickly drifted off. A cold, unmovable lump had settled in the pit of my stomach as I watched her sleep. For hours, I had contemplated how she could have known about the other accident. I had theories ranging from her overhearing my parents' conversations to thinking that I must talk in my sleep. But the most logical explanation I could come up with was that she was a kid, and anyone who had spent time with kids knows that they say weird things. So I had forced myself to settle back down and close my eyes.

In the light of day, it had been easy to push off the moment and the sensation it created. So I had. I had thrown myself to the mundane tasks of the day and by the time night had fallen again I had forgotten about it. I remember that the night had possessed a lingering chill and so quiet that I could hear my every breath. I had been comfortable and loose-limbed with sleep when the familiar creak of the door caught my attention. On instinct, I had reached back and patted the space behind me, beckoning Kimberly to come in like I had so many times before.

"Hello, little love."

My stomach had lurched into my throat at Kimberly's whisper. For a moment, in the thick blanket of the night, her voice had sounded just like the man's. I hadn't even known until that moment that I knew his voice. That I would be able to identify it. But I had. I bolted up and flicked on the bedside lamp. The soft glow had been enough to see Kimberly lingering in the doorway. She had just stood there watching me, a large dimpled smile on her face.

It had taken a few moments for me to find my voice and ask, "What did you just call me?"

I was only met with silence and a cold, vacant stare. My voice cracked as I screamed her name. But she hadn't flinched. She had blinked rapidly and toddled over to the bed. It had taken her a few attempts to crawl up and I hadn't tried to help her. Hadn't moved at all as she resumed her normal position pressed up against my side. After a moment, she reached out a tiny hand, hit me lightly, and groaned for me to turn off the light. I followed her command and we had plummeted into the shadows of the night.

Breakfast the next day had been eaten in awkward silence. I hadn't anticipated that such a slight incident could throw me off so completely. But every hair on my body stood on end at even the littlest reminder of that man. I didn't know how to deal with it. I didn't tell my parents. They kept their own demons from me so it only seemed fair to return the favor. And after all, what could I have possibly said?

But as much as we had all tried to keep to our own, Kimberly had noticed the mounting tension. She had been quiet that morning, her little shoulders hunched, and eyes fixed on her cereal. The sight had made guilt slither through my stomach. None of this was her fault.

The car had still been in the shop, so my parents were forced to carpool to work, leaving Kimberly and myself to make our own way to school. It wasn't a long walk, and I resolved that today we could cut through the park. Kimberly had liked the flowers and I decided that any trouble we got in for being late would be worth it to relieve some of the tension. Kimberly had brightened the second I told her of my plan. She had slid from her chair and disappeared into her room to collect her schoolbag. I had been rinsing the dishes in the sink when she called out to me and I didn't bother to turn as I responded.

I could feel her behind me, standing in the doorway of the kitchen. For a long moment, she was silent and I had thought she might have been waiting for me to turn around. Then she spoke, her voice soft but far more serious than I had ever heard her.

"I won't ever chew on your bones. I promise."

I had whirled on her, uncaring about the water that sloshed over the tiles. Our eyes had met, my heart hammering while her face remained a placid mask. Without another word, she had turned and walked out of the room.

My mind had swirled as I waited for her that afternoon. Logically, I knew it was crazy to put that much thought into the ramblings of a child. Most of the time, I doubted even she knew what she was saying. But each similarity had dug into my brain like spikes and I couldn't get them out. It didn't seem like she knew, fully at least, what had happened to me. But she already knew far more than I had ever wanted her to learn.

I will always remember Kimberly's happy squeal as she barreled out of the school and threw her tiny form into my arms. Her hair smelt of strawberry shampoo and was like thin silk as she held her tight. I might have held her too long because she had grown impatient and had tried to squirm out of my arms. I had smiled at her protests, having the passing thought that in a few more years she wouldn't want me to hug her at all, and had taken her schoolbag.

The walk home had been familiar, with Kimberly prattling on about everything she had learnt that day and presenting me each of her drawings with pride. I hadn't known half the kids she talked about, but that didn't stop her from glossing over everything like I had all the facts and past history at my disposal. It was impossible to understand what she was talking about and not really worth trying. So I had just nodded on occasion and tuned out the rest. Dozens of people had been waiting for the lights to change and we joined the crush. Our parents had long since hammered into us that we shouldn't cross the street without holding hands, so without a word we had blindly reached for one another.

The hand that had slid over my palm hadn't been the tiny limb I knew. It had been large, thick, and strong. The skin had scraped against my palm like sandpaper. It was a man's hand. I wrenched back. I searched the crowd for the man that had just gripped my fingers. But no one was paying attention to me. No one had been close enough, or old enough, to be responsible. Finally, I had looked down at Kimberly, finding her watching me with a furrowed brow.

"Daddy says you have to hold my hand," she had said.

I had assured her that I knew that, but she had just balled her little hands on her hips and asked why I had let go. The lights had changed and the crowd started to move. So I had placed a hand on the back of her head and rushed her across the street. She had protested the entire time that I didn't take her hand again.

The second we had gotten home, I had locked myself in my room. Kimberly called me a name and said I was being mean, but I had refused to come back out and I hadn't let her in. Time had helped me catch my breath. I couldn't push down the sickening feeling that had crawled up my throat. The event had rolled in my mind, but I couldn't find a way to explain any of this to my parents. My attempts just polished the memories until it was impossible to ignore them.

Dinner had been tense. Kimberly wouldn't stop staring at me. I couldn't read her expression anymore and it made the whole situation worse. As soon as I was allowed, I ran back to the safety of my room. The only words I managed to choke out to Kimberly was that she couldn't sleep in my bed tonight. She had protested and whined, effectively making me feel like a horrible human being. More than once I wanted to give in, but then I would remember the echoed words, the feel of that hand against my skin, and my resolve sharpened. I had gone to bed early that night but sleep didn't come for hours.

I still don't know what had woken me. It wasn't a sound or a touch, but I had startled awake all the same. Kimberly had been standing by my bed, a few inches from my face, watching me. Shrouded by shadows, she had stood as unmoving as stone, her large eyes unblinking. I had watched her back, muscles clenched until they ached.

Finally, I had managed to ask her what she was doing, but she had given me no response, no sign that she had even heard me at all. She had only stared. I swallowed and noticed that she was hiding something behind her back.

"Kimberly?" I had asked.

Her face had twitched and she had shifted her arms.

I had tried to keep my voice stern and sharp as I pressed, "What have you got behind your back?"

"Nothing," she replied innocently as she swayed her shoulders.

I didn't believe her and demanded that she show me. A smile had stretched across her face. That smile had sent shivers of fear slithering along my spine. For one heart-stopping moment, a slip of light caught the moonlight, then the bed rocked. I had thought she had just hit the bed, but in the dull light of the room, I saw something stuck into my bed. Kimberly hadn't moved. She had stood there, watching me as I watched her, my heart hammering in my throat. Then I had reached for the light and she had bolted from the room. In the bright light, I had been able to see that Kimberly had slammed a six-inch kitchen knife into the mattress a few inches from my head. It had been stabbed into the mattress with enough force to keep it upright.

I remember screaming. I remember my parents bursting into my room. But everything else that followed is shrouded in my mind. Kimberly's bedroom was empty. The front door was open. My parents still believe that she was taken, but I can't help but wonder if she ran.

It's been eight years, but those few days still consume my thoughts. I have yet to make any sense of what I had seen, what I had experienced. Had Kimberly been haunted by the man that had tried to kill me? Was it possible that he had come back, had been rebirthed as my sister to finish what he had started? That she had ran rather than hurt me? Or had my subconscious been screaming at me to notice that a predator was circling Kimberly and it had all gotten jumbled with my own past? I'm not sure I'll ever really know. But I pray every day that my sister will come back. And I'm terrified that one day she will.

* * *

Scarecrow
By A.I. Nasser

The first time my father hit me was the night my mother left.

I remember it like it was yesterday. His bloodshot eyes, the disturbing smile plastered on his face and the spittle on his lips from all the shouting. And of course, the belt. I don't think I could ever erase the memory of that piece of leather as he raised it high over his head and brought it down in a burning slap across my bare arms.

My mother had usually been around to protect Alice and me. She was our rock against the storm that was my old man, and his temper that was prone to exploding whenever we did anything stupid. It didn't take much to stop him, either. A simple threat of taking away the farm, a massive one hundred acre space of land that she had inherited from her own father, was enough to stop my old man from carrying out his ruthless punishments.

Looking back at it now, I believe I had really taken advantage of that, more than Alice had. It was easy to get away with things, and there was no love left between my parents for my mother to ever take his side. I never knew what had torn them apart, when the turning point in their twenty-year relationship had come, but it didn't matter to me then. For a pubescent boy whose father couldn't discipline, my mother was my 'get out of jail free' card, and I abused it.

Three weeks after my thirteenth birthday, I guess she had just had enough of it all. I can still picture her last night at home, how she sat in her chair out on the porch, sipping her usual lemon ice tea and pretending that I didn't know it was something stronger.

"Off to bed, Garfield," she teased. She poked me in the belly that had awarded me the nickname, and despite the urge to remind her how much I hated being likened to an orange cat, that night I had let it slide. Sometimes, I look back and wonder if maybe I should have spent a little more time with her on the porch. Maybe I would have known what she was up to and could have talked her out of it.

But I didn't stay with her, and the next morning she was gone.

"Women are like that," I remember my father telling me while he rummaged through their closet, looking for God knows what. "They're never satisfied. Now go wash your face and stop acting like a friggin' baby!"

He was never going to answer the multitude of questions swimming through my head, and Alice wasn't much help, either. Our mother's departure had obviously hit her hard, and she spent most of the day numb to anything and everything around her.

When she burned dinner, my father took his frustration out on her. I instantly regretted trying to stop him when the beatings began, and although they probably lasted only a few minutes, it felt like hours. It was almost as if he were beating me for every single mistake I had ever done, making up for the years my mother had stood up to him.

I think back to the weeks that followed that particular day, and sometimes wish he had killed me then and there.

***

The scarecrow came a week later.

By then, the days had begun merging together, each the same as the other, until I really couldn't tell when one had ended and the next began. At some point, I had to check the calendar just to make sure my mind wasn't playing tricks on me, that a day truly had ended. It was proof that the sleepless nights I was experiencing, cowering under the covers while my father stomped around the house, drunk and angry, were finally over.

The old man had started a reign of terror in our household. There was no telling what would set him off anymore; the smallest things igniting a fire so furious, he would burst into a blinding rage and a barrage of beatings. He would wake me at odd hours just to satisfy his urges, shouting and slapping until I was huddled in a corner with my hands up in defense and tears streaming down my face. The rising and setting of the sun was not enough to let me know that I had survived another day.

But, if I thought I had it bad, and back then I truly believed I did, then Alice had been living a nightmare. She had quickly been promoted to taking care of the things my mother had once been responsible for. However, without the threat of losing the farm, my father could voice his disapproval a lot more physically than he had before. Some nights, I could hear Alice crying in the room beside mine, and although I would want to go and comfort her, I never could find the courage to do it. Other nights, I would cower in my bed, shaking and sweating, as my father stomped passed the closed door to my room and barged into hers. She would scream of course, shrill at times, muffled at others, and I could clearly hear the slaps my father would administer to shut her up. Whatever he was doing in there, the few minutes of listening to my sister's screams and my father's grunts seemed like a lifetime, and to this day, they haunt my dreams.

The scarecrow was the only thing that seemed to break the cycle.

I didn't know where it had come from, or why my father had suddenly decided that we needed one, but it looked horrific. The first time I laid eyes upon it, strolling out the back door and onto the small yard between the house and the corn fields, it had stopped me cold and sent chills up and down my back. About fifty yards in the distance, crucified for eternity, it hung over the stalks of corn and stared right at me.

I knew the notion was absurd, that there was no merit to how I felt the first time I saw that damn thing out in the fields. But those days, my emotions were in complete control over my mind, and no logical part of me ever considered speaking up and correcting the ludicrous imaginations of a teenage child. A pile of hay covered in my father's old clothes and my mother's Sunday hat. Still, I could swear those eyes were directed right at me, watching me, the smile drawn across its face with a black marker aimed in my direction.

Come out into the fields, Garfield. Just a little closer so I can tell you the funniest thing you will ever hear. I have a few secrets to share, and I'm sure you're going to want to hear

74

them. Want to know why Alice screams at night? Definitely not beatings, kiddo.

I decided to stop venturing out into the back yard after that.

***

I don't remember exactly when the nightmares began, but I do remember it was after Alice was taken to the hospital.

My sister had fallen into complete silence by then, going about her chores with the numbness of a psych patient. She was on cruise control, working off instinct rather than actually paying attention to what it was she was doing, and even when I would try talking to her, she would just look at me with an empty gaze. Whatever was left of her, whatever could still be labeled as Alice, was lost somewhere deep behind those eyes, locked away in a corner where my father couldn't get to. To me, she had slowly become nothing more than a walking corpse, and although it broke my heart to see her that way, there was very little I could do.

It was the laundry, I think, that lead to the beating. Alice had forgotten to empty out the pockets of my father's jeans and had washed the three hundred dollars there with the rest of the clothes. I had never seen my father that angry, and once the beating started, it took a very dangerous turn, quickly. Alice had apparently become numb to my father's strikes as well, and the more she stayed quiet, the more she failed to react with every slap, punch and kick, the angrier he got.

It all came to a shuddering halt when he grabbed her by the back of her head and slammed her face into the wall. The sheer volume of blood that was pouring out of her broken nose was enough to make me gag, and equally enough to snap my father out of his blind outburst. There were a few awful seconds of complete silence only broken by Alice's gasps for air, coughing and sputtering, the blood seeping into the front of her shirt and turning her white blouse a dark crimson.

"Don't you move!" my father shouted at me, suddenly overtaken by urgency as he raced about the living room and grabbed his coat.

75

They were out of the house in minutes, driving away just as the sun was setting and a soft wind began to pick up around the house. I watched from the front porch, my hands buried deep in my pockets, and for the first time since my mother had left, I contemplated running away. I had thought of it before, especially after the worst beatings, but always knew that somehow my father would find me, and the consequences would be severe.

Now, though, I had a head start. He would be far too busy making excuses at the hospital for Alice's broken nose, and I would have the perfect window of opportunity to escape. I had some money stowed away, enough for a one-way ticket to wherever the hell I wanted. I had no idea where to go, or what I would do once I got there, but that didn't matter. What was important was getting away from here forever.

I raced up the stairs to my room, closing the door behind me out of habit than anything else, the sounds of the empty house a bit too ominous for my liking. A few of the lights had burned out over the past week or so, and my father still hadn't gotten around to changing them. The dimmer illumination left shadows were none had been before, and it only made my urgency to leave stronger. I couldn't stay in this godforsaken place any longer.

Thoughts of Alice suddenly crossed my mind, and the fear of what might happen to her if I left filled me. I stood motionless by the small desk near my window, my hands on the open drawer where two hundred dollars hid beneath my science book, awaiting to be retrieved and used. I couldn't do it. I couldn't leave her behind with that monster where his fury would go unchecked. This time he broke her nose; there was no telling what he might do next.

The wind whistled through the window, and I closed the door with a shaking hand, frustrated and angry, knowing that I would forever be stuck in this house as long as that madman walked around freely. I thought of calling the police, but my father wasn't stupid, and he would somehow find a way out of trouble.

My mind raced with possible solutions, but nothing seemed promising enough. I reached out to close the window

76

over my desk, glancing briefly at the corn fields behind the house, when I froze in horror.

The scarecrow was perched in the backyard, hanging from its crucifix at an angle that allowed its hollow eyes to stare up at my window, its black smile wider.

***

I didn't sleep that night, hiding under my bed even when I heard my father's truck drive up to the house and the sounds of Alice's soft footsteps walking up the stairs and into her room. I don't remember when I had finally fallen asleep, but I woke up with a start when my father pounded on my bedroom door, stormed into the room and pulled me out from under the bed.

"Did you move it?" he was shouting. "You good-for-nothing piece of shit, did you move it?"

He shook me so violently, my teeth rattled in my head, and my words came out in stutters and gasps. He grabbed me by the collar of my shirt and dragged me downstairs and out to the back. I fought him, unable to break free of his grip but terrified enough to know that I didn't want to be anywhere near that damned thing.

The scarecrow was watching me with a smile, and when I looked up at it, now upright as if it hadn't just been laughing at me last night, I felt my heartbeat race to a painfully thundering pounding in my chest.

"You carry it, then!" my father was screaming. "You think you're funny? Big clown, huh? You're going to carry it all the way back, or God help me, I'll string you up right next to it!"

I carried it, and it was the longest twenty minutes of my life.

To this day, I remember the splinters that punctured my skin as my father forced me to pull it out of the ground with my bare hands. I remember trying not to look up at its horrid face and that awful smile as I leaned it onto my back. I remember the heaviness of it, as if I were carrying a sack of rocks instead of strands of hay. I remember my father barking orders as the sun's rays beat down at me while I set the scarecrow back down in its regular place.

The worst of it all was the feel of the hay against my skin, the straws stroking the nape of my neck and the wind blowing through the corn stalks as if the damn thing were breathing against me. I could imagine its smile behind me, its eyes boring into the back of my head, and for a split second, I imagined its hands breaking loose from their ropes and wrapping around my neck, choking me to death as I carried it.

My father didn't string me up next to it, but he did use his belt. And all the while, my eyes kept seeing the scarecrow's face on his, laughing manically as I cried out with every strike.

***

Alice didn't come out of her room the whole day, and I found myself suddenly responsible for her chores. I think I gained a newfound respect for her after only a few hours doing what she had to do every day. Of course, my father was always there, breathing down my neck, quick with a slap across the back of my head when he wasn't satisfied.

But none of that fazed me. The memory of the scarecrow in the backyard and the chore of carrying it back to its spot had left a lingering feeling of dread inside me, stronger than anything my father could say or do. Suddenly it felt like the walls of the house were closing in on me, as if I were being boxed in with no prospects of escaping.

At night, I could hear Alice crying through the thin wall separating our rooms, and a part of me felt like I was abandoning her, even though I was only a few feet away. I had no idea if I could comfort her, if anything I said could make up for the abuse she was experiencing, and I was too scared to try.

I heard my father's heavy footsteps climbing the stairs, and closed my eyes when he passed by my room and into Alice's. Within minutes, the grunting began, and although I tried to block it out, it kept me awake until it stopped. Alice's bedroom door opened and closed, and I listened as my father made his way back downstairs.

Scarecrow

I climbed out of bed, shaking with fury, angered at my helplessness, and ventured back to my desk and secret stash. The money would be enough for both me and Alice. I could get us out of here, away from the farm and my father. There was enough for two tickets, and I was sure that once far away, Alice would return to her usual self and we could both find a way to live out the rest of our lives without any problems.

I looked up at my window, feeling my body being drawn to it slowly, dreading what I might see once I looked outside. I knew that the logical thing to do was crawl back into bed and try to sleep, but some sick and twisted part of me wanted to take a peek and make sure that what had happened last night had not been repeated. I needed to believe that it had been some sick joke played by a couple of drunken teenagers looking for a good time. The alternative was too horrible to fathom.

I walked to the window in small, tentative steps, and as I drew closer, I could already see the corn field beyond, and the absence of the scarecrow from its crucifix. My eyes scanned the backyard, goose bumps breaking out all across my skin and a cold finger tracing a line down my spine.

When I finally found the scarecrow, it was lying on the step of the back porch, its face towards the sky and its hollow eyes staring straight at me.

***

I didn't wait for a beating. At dawn, when there was just enough sunlight to assure that the shadows had been dispersed, but not enough to wake my father, I went out and carried the scarecrow back. I went through the motions quickly, my eyes fixated on the destination as I tried my best to ignore the straws poking out and stabbing into my arms. It was heavier than the last time, and after a few steps, I dropped it onto the ground and dragged it through the corn the rest of the way. It took me almost half an hour to take the stake down, tie the scarecrow back on, and pull the whole thing back upright. By the end of it, the muscles in my back were screaming bloody murder.

79

I hurried through the morning chores, fixing breakfast just as my father walked into the kitchen. I braced myself as he stared at his eggs and bacon with clear disgust before grunting and beginning to eat.

"Don't," he hissed at me when I took a second plate and made my way towards the stairs.

"She needs to eat," I replied.

My father only had to look up from his food, and I trudged back to the kitchen table and sat down opposite him.

If I had known it was his last day alive, I might have acted differently.

***

I remember seventh grade English class, when my teacher was discussing a fantastical story about a boy who spent every night in the attic of an abandoned house playing with Elves and fairies. The story was told from the point of view of the boy as an adult man returning to his childhood home, and how his memories turned out to be nothing more than a child's imagination. When I look back at the night my father died, I wonder just how much of it was imagination, and how much was real.

The day my father decided that Alice would not be fed, sitting at the kitchen table and eating his breakfast, was the day my entire world was turned upside down. It was also one of the rare days he didn't beat me just for the hell of it, although there was one moment in the late afternoon when I thought he would stick his fist all the way down my throat.

I avoided Alice's room like a plague, my mind selfishly content and excited that I would possibly go through twenty-four hours without having to endure my father's wrath. When I finally closed my bedroom door and crawled under the covers, a part of me sighed with relief. There might have even been a smile on my face, although that's one detail I could never remember.

Everything else that happened that night is etched in my memory forever.

It started with my father's usual trips to Alice's room, the stomping of heavy feet on the stairs and down the hallway, the creaking of a door opening and the slamming sound of it closing again. And, of course, the grunts.

Although Alice had come to fall silent during the past few visits, that night her screams were shrill enough to make me jump up in bed and my heart beat like a hammer in my chest. Fists slammed against the wall over my head, and for a moment, I truly believed I would see hands break through from the other side. I jumped out of bed hurriedly, stepping back and away from the screaming and the pounding, from the angry shouts of my father and the sound of hard slaps coming from across the wall.

My body shook uncontrollably, and my eyes stared in horror at the wall separating my room from Alice's. Her screams cut through the still night as if she were right there in my bed, kicking and lashing out at the man who had been abusing her for the past weeks. I felt frozen in place, unable to do anything more than listen to the sounds of my sister's screams.

Something hard slammed against the wall, and Alice's screams stopped. In the sudden silence that followed, my beating heart was like a drum in my ears, and I fought hard not to race out of my room and into the night, away from the house and the horrors within.

That was when Alice's door creaked open, and through the wall, a shuffle of sheets and a flutter of feet followed.

"What is this?" I heard my father say, his voice muffled, clearly out of breath. "Is this some kind of joke? How did you get inside my house?"

I felt a chill race through me, and for some inexplicable reason, I rushed across the bedroom and to the window. I gazed out at the corn fields, squinting to see through the fog that had begun to settle around the house, and knew what I would see before I saw it.

The scarecrow was missing.

The sounds of my father screaming froze the blood in veins. I had never heard a man's cries of pain and terror so shrill before, and as I stared out of my window, my eyes fixated on the empty crucifix where the scarecrow should have been, the screams turned into gurgling gasps of agony followed by the sickening sound of breaking bones.

A heavy thump followed, and the house fell into complete silence for a few seconds before I heard the sound of Alice's door opening and closing, and the approaching sounds of soft footsteps. I didn't turn around, my eyes gazing straight ahead through the window, my body beginning to shake uncontrollably. The footsteps stopped just outside my door, and through the reflection in the window, I watched in horror as the knob turned and the door swung open slowly.

The scarecrow trudged into my room and stopped once it was a few feet inside. I couldn't turn, praying that if I stayed completely still, it might realize I was harmless and leave me alone. I had no idea what it had done to my father, but my imagination ran wild with the lingering sounds I had been forced to hear just minutes before. My eyes were locked onto the reflection of the holes of its eyes, and for a quick instant, I saw a flicker of movement there. The hat on its head hung askew, and between the straws, I could see golden strands of blonde hair matted with mud.

It spoke, and although its voice was horrifyingly muffled, as if it had swallowed sand and was trying to speak through mouthfuls of it, there was a tone there that I recognized.

"Off to bed, Garfield. He won't hurt you anymore."

***

They found me out in the corn fields, unconscious and shaking.

The doctors called it conversion disorder, a result of the severe stress, and it took me years before I could finally speak and answer anyone's questions. They kept me isolated most of the time, and it was only after I was able to communicate properly did I find out what had become of my family.

Alice was dead, beaten so badly that the damage to her organs and the internal bleeding were enough to make sure she had found a permanent escape from the clutches of our father. I miss her, and sometimes wish I could find some way to tell her 'I'm sorry,' that there was no excuse for my cowardice when I should have been rushing to save her.

The monster that had been my father was found dead from multiple stab wounds. The police told me that most of the bones in his body had been shattered by what appeared to be a baseball bat. If the stabbing hadn't killed him, the bleeding would have. They had found both weapons in the corn field as well.

My mother had never left, either. She was found covered in hay and old clothes, hanging from a crucifix in the middle of the corn field, hidden in plain sight. She had been strangled to death weeks before, most probably by my father, and the police asked me several questions about their relationship in her last few days, before giving up completely when I started to scream.

I never really recovered from what happened, from what I saw. Until now, I still wake up screaming, locked away in my padded room, the effects of the medication wearing off faster every night. Sometimes, when the lights are out and the illumination from the hall outside isn't enough to scare the shadows away, I can see the scarecrow standing in a corner, watching me with its hollow eyes. And each time it would speak to me.

"Off to bed, Garfield."

* * *

Graveyard Shift
By Ron Ripley

Allen had worked at five separate nursing homes prior to taking a maintenance position at the Ray Chandler Home in Hingham, Massachusetts. He had also been let go from each of the previous five establishments.

Not fired. No, never fired, Allen thought, grinning. *Too careful for that to happen.*

His grin spread to a smile as he filled the mop bucket with hot water. Bubbles foamed directly beneath the heavy flow from the spigot in the custodian's closet, the strong, comforting smell of cleanser filling the small room.

While the water level rose in the bucket, Allen quickly glanced out the doorway. When he saw no one was around, he ducked back in and checked his stash.

In an old laundry detergent bottle marked clearly with the words, "Vomit Cleaner" on masking tape, Allen hid his gems. His extra source of income. The pain meds he swiped from the residents. Mostly muscle-relaxers, mixed with the occasional oxy. He was never heavy-handed, only stealing one or two each shift. Any more and people would notice.

They figure it out eventually anyway, Allen thought, tucking the 'Vomit Cleaner' back down behind a stack of one-ply toilet paper rolls. He turned off the water, carefully backed out into the hall as he held onto the smooth handle of the mop, and looked around.

Two in the morning on the graveyard shift and the fourth floor was quiet.

Perfect, Allen thought.

When it was quiet, he usually could find his insurance. The reason why he'd been let go but never fired.

No, he grinned. *Never fired. Not Allen Wells.*

In the quiet hours of the morning, when even the worst insomniacs had gone to sleep, the nurses and staff showed they were worse than a group of hormone-riddled teens at a boy-girl sleepover.

Allen had caught plenty of people in compromising situations. And never with their spouses. Allen always made a big production out of the discovery, too.

Oh! I'm so sorry, he would say. *This is so embarrassing!*

He would scurry out of the room or office. He never took pictures. Pictures could be seen as evidence of blackmail.

He smiled and thought, *Who needs pictures? They live in fear of me telling their husband or wife. Fear of me going to the press and saying, I was fired 'cause I caught Nurse Nancy with Doctor Dan!*

The idea of it made him chuckle. Any sort of investigation would show he didn't use the pills he stole but sold them instead. He had a different addiction, a problem with horses and how they ran.

I never pick a winner, Allen sighed, shaking his head.

He didn't want to go to the papers. It would have been bad for everyone. Better to quietly suggest they let him go.

They always did.

And he always got another job.

Janitors were in high demand at nursing homes.

No matter how much you clean, Allen thought, stopping at the nurse's station, *you can never get the smell of death out of the air.*

"Hey, Allen," Mary Beth said, coming out of the back of the station.

"Hey yourself," Allen said, grinning. He put the mop in the wringer, squeezed it out and began to clean around the desk. He liked Mary Beth. She never gave him a hard time about his job, so he always took care of her area first.

She stifled a yawn and asked, "Did they tell you Dr. Chandler was coming in to do rounds at three?"

Allen paused, saying, "No."

"He is," Mary Beth said. "You may want to take your break then. He's a little different. Katya Denisovich, the first shift supervisor, she'll be in here with him. I'm taking my break when they show up. You're welcome to join me."

"Thanks," Allen said, "but I've got to leave early, so no break for me. Just a quick cigarette. But I'll take it at three, to be on the safe side."

"Alright, Allen," Mary Beth said. She yawned again, shook her head and started to work on the computer.

Allen whistled to himself as he mopped the floor. He moved steadily away from the nurse's station.

Dr. Chandler's coming in, Allen thought happily. *And with the head nurse. At three. Three in the morning.*

Sometimes, he thought, whistling a little louder, *it's just too easy.*

For nearly an hour, Allen worked steadily. Attempting to clean the uncleanable. At 2:55 a.m., Mary Beth found him.

"You may want to grab that cigarette now, Allen," she said softly. "They're here."

"Thanks," he said, pushing the mop and bucket into a corner by a fire door. "I'll grab my smokes and be outside."

She nodded. "Do yourself a favor. Stay out there until you see them leave, alright? It's best to give them their 'alone time'."

"Sure thing."

Mary Beth smiled, glanced nervously back towards the center of the wing and then left.

Allen wandered back to the custodian's closet and went in and got his cigarettes and lighter out of his coat pocket. He made sure to pass by the nurse's station so he could get a look at the lovebirds.

They were the oddest couple he had ever seen.

Katya Denisovich was middle-aged, shorter than average, and she looked as though she could have worked in a circus as a strongman. Her face was broad, slightly tanned, and topped with platinum blonde hair kept in a neat bun at the back of her head.

Dr. Chandler was the polar opposite.

He was tall, almost freakishly so, and looked as though he would hit his head if he didn't duck when he passed through a doorway. His skin was exceptionally pale and seemed as though it was paper thin. His arms and legs were longer than they should have been, bare wrists showing where his shirt-sleeves ended. He was bald, too, and his skull was slightly elongated, almost coming to a point in the back.

I might have to take pictures of this, Allen thought gleefully as he kept a solemn expression on his face. *Bet I could sell them to some dirty website.*

He smiled at the curious couple, received near simultaneous nods in reply, and made his way to the elevator. He rode it down to the ground floor, hurried over to the service elevator and took it to the third floor.

The trick, he reminded himself, *was to be quick and quiet.*

From the third floor, he took the back stairs to the fourth and slipped out onto the wing. He stood in the corner by his mop and bucket and listened.

It won't be long now, he thought.

Over the years, Allen had learned how to be patient. So he waited, and he listened.

Soon he heard them, the noises coming from Mr. Gunderson's room.

Allen sighed, disgusted.

Poor Mr. G, he thought. *The old man has the room to himself, and they do it in there while he's sleeping?*

He shook the disgusted feeling off and crept along the hall to Mr. Gunderson's room. Mr. Wilkins, Gunderson's former roommate, had passed away the week before. People usually got new roommates quickly, but not Mr. Gunderson.

Bet this is why, Allen thought, nearing the open door. *So they can have their little meetings. Guy's on so many meds, he'd never notice what they're up to.*

Allen stopped at the placard under the room number and listened. One of the room's beds creaked and groaned. Someone was panting and moaning, the bed occasionally slamming into the wall.

A smile moved across Allen's face, and he quickly got it under control. It wouldn't do to look like the cat who caught the canary, not when he needed to pretend surprise. Allen took a deep breath, allowed a mask of innocence to slip over his face, and he stepped into the doorway.

"I'm sorry," Allen started, but the rest of the sentence died in his mouth. The scene before him robbed him of the ability to speak. Almost of the power to think.

Mr. Gunderson was on his bed, the blankets thrown off and lying in a heap on the linoleum floor. His flannel pajama shirt was torn open, the buttons shining in the pale light of the bed table's lamp. Pale skin, splashed with dark red blood, greeted Allen's eyes, as did the sight of Katya Denisovich perched on the old man's frail legs.

Her hands were wrist deep in Mr. Gunderson's open stomach, some unknown organ held lovingly in front of her. The same blood which stained the old man's flesh was spread around her lips, the muscles in her jaw moving steadily as she chewed her grim food.

And Katya was looking at Allen. Her eyes were a brilliant, breathtaking blue and Allen found he couldn't look away from her.

She swallowed, took another bite of the recently deceased Mr. Gunderson's inner works, and never took her gaze from Allen.

Run, he told himself. His legs wouldn't obey.

Turn around and run, he commanded.

His body refused, and he remained perfectly still, unable to move or stop watching the horror before him.

The whisper of a footstep reminded him of Dr. Chandler.

The tall man ducked his head and stepped out of the darkened bathroom. He looked curiously at Allen, and then to Katya.

The doctor's voice was deep and grating as he spoke to the woman, the words unintelligible, a language Allen had never heard before.

Katya nodded, placed the remnants of the organ on Mr. Gunderson's thin chest, and climbed down. Dr. Chandler's large hand wrapped firmly around Allen's bicep, and suddenly Allen was walking. His steps were mechanical, obeying someone else's command.

He was marched drunkenly to the bedside of the late Mr. Gunderson and forced to stand in front of Katya. The woman picked up a wet-wipe from the bed table, tore the small package open and removed the thin, soft paper from within. In silence, she unfolded it, the sharp smell of the cleanser stinging Allen's nose.

With careful, delicate movements she cleaned the blood from her face and hands. Finally, she deposited the wipe upon the organ and looked at Allen.

"Well," she said, smiling at him, "this is quite the predicament we find ourselves in, is it not?"

Allen wanted to answer, but found he couldn't.

"No," Katya said, "you can't answer me. I don't want you to. I've heard enough whining from the likes of you for one day. The amount of prattling you all do is mind-numbing."

Dr. Chandler asked her a question in their strange language, and she nodded, smiling.

"My *familiar* is quite concerned about you," Katya said, walking to Mr. Gunderson's easy chair and sitting down. "It has been decades since someone was so rude as to walk in on me. He is wondering what we are to do with you. I'm sure you're wondering the same."

Just let me go! Allen wanted to shout. *I won't say a word, I promise!*

"I'm certain," Katya continued, "that right now you're saying you'll keep your mouth shut. And I do believe you, by the way. You are, quite frankly, rank with fear. I know when someone tells the truth, and when they don't. When they mean what they say, and whether or not they'll be able to do what they promise. And you, Allen, you mean what you say, and you would do it as well."

Oh thank God, Allen said. Tears welled up in his eyes, and he felt joy and relief rush through him simultaneously.

"That being said," she said, smiling, "I'm not letting you go."

A cold wall of fear slammed into Allen.

"No, not at all. Because of your 'modern' society, I am forced to feed on the likes of this," she said, gesturing towards Mr. Gunderson's corpse. "Younger, though not necessarily fresher meat is so rarely available to me. And to think that Baba Yaga has been brought down so low."

Dr. Chandler spoke, and she shrugged.

"It doesn't matter if he knows my name or not," she said, sighing as she stood up. "I'll be having his tongue for breakfast. Bring him home, my dear, I shall see you as soon as I've finished my dinner."

Panic swarmed over Allen and he turned. Dr. Chandler stood directly behind him. The man's pale face was emotionless. Expressionless. His features were masklike, no more real than a child's Halloween costume.

With his heart thundering in his chest, Allen tried to run past the man. Dr. Chandler's great hands were too fast, a blur of movement and Allen was slapped backward. He spun, smashed into the wall, staggered and fell into Mr. Gunderson's bureau. Pictures tumbled, a frame fell and the glass smashed on the cold floor.

Allen slipped off of the edge of the bureau, a throbbing pain exploding in his hip. He caught himself as he dropped down, screaming as glass cut into the palms of his hands and the tips of his fingers.

Still he struggled to get to his feet, his mind racing. He could no longer think coherently, his eyes locking onto the steady drip of blood from Mr. Gunderson's bed.

Baba Yaga's tall, strange familiar stepped closer and Allen weakly swung a lacerated hand towards him.

The woman laughed, spoke in the curious language, and her tall familiar responded with a foot to Allen's ribs.

Allen gagged, bile springing into his mouth, his ribs breaking beneath the force of the blow. He dropped painfully to the floor, glass cutting deeply into his face.

Seconds later, Allen felt himself being picked up easily by Dr. Chandler, the strange man cradling him against his chest. For the first time, he realized the doctor was cold to the touch, and that there was no heartbeat to hear beneath the man's breast.

Oh, Christ, Allen thought, *oh, Jesus Christ. What have I done? I didn't mean it. I didn't mean any of it. Christ almighty, it isn't worth this!*

The sounds of Baba Yaga's feast filled his ears and Allen, gasping for breath and unable to move or scream, wept as he was carried from the room.

* * *

90

FREE Bonus Novel!

Wow, I hope you enjoyed this book as much as I did writing it! If you enjoyed the book, please leave a review. Your reviews inspire me to continue writing about the world of spooky and untold horrors!

To really show you my appreciation for purchasing this book, please enjoy a **FREE extra spooky bonus novel.** This will surely leave you running scared!

Visit below to download your bonus novel and to learn about my upcoming releases, future discounts and giveaways: www.ScareStreet.com

FREE books (30 - 60 pages):
Ron Ripley (Ghost Stories)
1. Ghost Stories (Short Story Collection)
   www.scarestreet.com/ghost

A.I. Nasser (Supernatural Suspense)
2. Polly's Haven (Short Story)
   www.scarestreet.com/pollys
3. This is Gonna Hurt (Short Story)
   www.scarestreet.com/thisisgonna

Multi-Author Scare Street Collaboration
4. Horror Stories: A Short Story Collection
   www.scarestreet.com/horror

And experience the full-length novels (150 – 210 pages):
Ron Ripley (Ghost Stories)
1. Sherman's Library Trilogy (FREE via mailing list signup)
   www.scarestreet.com
2. The Boylan House Trilogy
   www.scarestreet.com/boylantri
3. The Blood Contract Trilogy
   www.scarestreet.com/bloodtri

4. The Enfield Horror Trilogy
   www.scarestreet.com/enfieldtri

Moving In Series

5. **Moving In Series Box Set Books 1 - 3 (22% off)**
   www.scarestreet.com/movinginbox123
6. Moving In (Book 1)
   www.scarestreet.com/movingin
7. The Dunewalkers (Moving In Series Book 2)
   www.scarestreet.com/dunewalkers
8. Middlebury Sanitarium (Book 3)
   www.scarestreet.com/middlebury
9. **Moving In Series Box Set Books 4 - 6 (25% off)**
   www.scarestreet.com/movinginbox456
10. The First Church (Book 4)
    www.scarestreet.com/firstchurch
11. The Paupers' Crypt (Book 5)
    www.scarestreet.com/paupers
12. The Academy (Book 6)
    www.scarestreet.com/academy

Berkley Street Series

13. Berkley Street (Book 1)
    www.scarestreet.com/berkley
14. The Lighthouse (Book 2)
    www.scarestreet.com/lighthouse
15. The Town of Griswold (Book 3)
    www.scarestreet.com/griswold
16. Sanford Hospital (Book 4)
    www.scarestreet.com/sanford
17. Kurkow Prison (Book 5)
    www.scarestreet.com/kurkow
18. Lake Nutaq (Book 6)
    www.scarestreet.com/nutaq
19. Slater Mill (Book 7)
    www.scarestreet.com/slater
20. Borgin Keep (Book 8)
    www.scarestreet.com/borgin
21. Amherst Burial Ground (Book 9)
    www.scarestreet.com/amherst

Hungry Ghosts Street Series

David Longhorn (Supernatural Suspense)
The Sentinels Series
37. Sentinels (Book 1)
   www.scarestreet.com/sentinels
38. The Haunter (Book 2)
   www.scarestreet.com/haunter
39. The Smog (Book 3)
   www.scarestreet.com/smog
Dark Isle Series
40. Dark Isle (Book 1)
   www.scarestreet.com/darkisle
41. White Tower (Book 2)
   www.scarestreet.com/whitetower
42. The Red Chapel (Book 3)
   www.scarestreet.com/redchapel
Ouroboros Series
43. The Sign of Ouroboros (Book 1)
   www.scarestreet.com/ouroboros
44. Fortress of Ghosts (Book 2)
   www.scarestreet.com/fortress
45. Day of The Serpent (Book 3)
   www.scarestreet.com/serpent
Curse of Weyrmouth Series
46. Curse of Weyrmouth (Book 1)
   www.scarestreet.com/weyrmouth
47. Blood of Angels (Book 2)
   www.scarestreet.com/bloodofangels

Eric Whittle (Psychological Horror)
Catharsis Series
48. Catharsis (Book 1)
   www.scarestreet.com/catharsis
49. Mania (Book 2)
   www.scarestreet.com/mania
50. Coffer (Book 3)
   www.scarestreet.com/coffer
Sara Clancy (Supernatural Suspense)
Dark Legacy Series

Keeping it spooky,
Team Scare Street

Printed in Great Britain
by Amazon